Be A Stand-Up Comic

(or just look like one)

Be A Stand-Up Comic

(or just look like one)

By Bob Stobener and R. Scott Edwards

Illustrations by Bob Stobener

Published by Laughs Unlimited Inc.
1124 Firehouse Alley
Sacramento, CA 95814

ISBN 0-9624792-0-9

Contents

The authors of this book wish to acknowledge and THANK
Garry Shandling
Bob Saget
Bruce Baum
Dave Coulier
George Wallace
and Tim Bedore
for it was these individuals which, in our humble beginnings,
helped and inspired us to make Laughs Unlimited in Sacramento
one of the country's longest running comedy club
operations.

Ten years on, we remain grateful for their help and friendship.

We would also like to thank the following people for their
contributions to this project: Kenny Aubrey, Diane Nichols, Mike
Larsen, Tim Wiggins and Ernie Olson.

Cover photo by Bentoni.

Foreword

This is a "how to" book. But rather than being a book about building a back yard shed or overhauling your car, this book is designed to help the budding young comedian (or comedienne). Stand-up comedy is one of the most popular forms of entertainment today. Yet, as the industry expands, one fact about performing comedy occasionally gets lost in the massive shuffle ... Comedy, especially Stand-Up Comedy, is a true Art Form.

We, the authors of this book, are comedy club owners. The more cynical readers might ask "what does a club owner know about comedy?" The question is worthy of discussion. Even though our experience is on the business side of the industry rather than the creative side, we have had the privilege of working with stand-up comics of every possible rank and level of expertise for nearly ten years! Through our work with these creative talents, we believe we have discovered many of the crucial points of development for stand-up comics. People who have thought about getting into comedy have often asked us how to make it in this business. Veteran comics have asked us as club owners what we're looking for so they can move up in their careers. Our answers are in this book.

Since comedy is an art form, and there are really no set rules in art, it becomes obvious that there are many ways to find success in comedy. This book, which takes a beginning comic through all of the steps of a comedy career, suggests several ideas which have proven successful for many of the biggest comics in the business. With the knowledge you'll gain from this book, along with your own enthusiasm and talent, we hope you'll find your own way to success.

Enjoy studying stand-up comedy and here's to your big laughs!

Chapter One
"I am a Funny Person"

You were a normal, happy everyday person living your life from day to day in a pleasant, peaceful existence. You went to school. You got a job. You made some money. Perhaps you bought a house. Maybe you even got married and started to settle down. But somewhere in this "All-American Dream" something went wrong. A passing comment by a friend, relative or acquaintance threw your comfortable lifestyle into a blazing inferno of trauma, trials and tribulations. A simple phrase uttered by an unsuspecting soul unleashed a secret desire in you to throw away everything you've worked for and turn your world upside down.

Someone told you you were funny!

Sometimes that's all it takes. In your personal circle of friends and relatives, you are possibly the world's funniest person. Forget those "Robin Williams, Richard Pryor" guys. YOU are a walking joke machine! That's when that dangerous thought process begins. In the darkest reaches of your mind, you begin to think "Hey! I AM funny! I can make my friends LAUGH! I bet I could make ANYBODY LAUGH! I see those guys on TV. They're not half as funny as me! Why can't I do that?! I know! I'll be a STAND-UP COMIC!!! I'll be a STAR! I'll be FAMOUS!! I'll be RICH!!! Those "Robin Williams, Richard Pryor" guys will be history after they see me!"

There is really nothing wrong with this kind of thinking. After all, motivation is a key ingredient in achieving any goal in life ... even performing stand-up comedy.

However, those initial dreams of comic success that motivate you into getting into this business of comedy can be inspiring ... or suicidal. The secret of survival is understanding the balance between your comedy dreams and reality. That's what this book is all about. We're going to show you the inside world of the comedy biz ... how it works and how to make money at it. We'll show you where to improve and what to look out for in the comedy jungles. We'll show you how to sell yourself to potential bookers. We will show you the reality that will keep your dreams of success in check. Perhaps with this knowledge and a lot of luck and talent, your odds of being one of those "Robin Williams, Richard Pryor" guys will get better.

Remember, someone told them they were funny once too.

OK let's start. You want to be a comic? You're crazy ... that's a good start. Let's measure you up and see if you are a naturally funny person. Not everyone is naturally funny and some people really have to work at it. Believe us!!! To begin with, let's examine your childhood and your up-bringing. It used to be a widely held notion that you had to be a victim of a terrible childhood to have a chance to be funny. Poverty, abuse, broken homes were all considered prerequisites of being an absolutely hilarious person. In some cases, this may have been true, but for the most part it's a myth. Yes, even if you happen to be rich, born of wealthy parents, and Republican, you too can make it in the world of comedy. Just don't walk to your car by yourself when you leave the club at night.

What were you like as a kid? Were you the class clown? Were you comfortable getting up in front of the class? Were you popular? If the answer is "yes" to all of the above, you may have the nucleus to be a funny adult. Then again, you may have the nucleus to be an overbearing, obnoxious jerk. However, if you began to see the absurdities in life at a young age and could present yourself well to others using a good form of communication, you were on the right track. If you couldn't, then you'd better take tomorrow off and start working on it.

What was your home life like? Was it "Leave It To Beaver" or "Divorce Court"? You folks on the "Divorce Court" side have the potential for comedy if you protected yourself from family tension by never taking anything too seriously. If you could get through all of your family's problems by crawling into your imagination and inventing a world of lighthearted nonsense, you very possibly built a personality trait in you that will greatly help you in comedy. If you could hide your emotional scars and bitterness by laughing at the world with a "nothing to lose" attitude, you are either hilarious or dangerous. Let's hope you're hilarious.

If you're from the "Leave It To Beaver" side, you basically owe everything in you that's funny to your parents, family, friends and home environment. If your parents were funny and enjoyed a good sense of humor, chances are you inherited it from them just like your big ears. Your parents play an important part in your early years as your chief role models and their personalities are often emulated by you. Don't worry if your parents weren't George and Gracie though. If they were strict disciplinarians with the sense of humor of a shoe, you still could have developed a talent for being funny. You just had to get it from somewhere else. Maybe your crazy Uncle Harrold who played old Bill Cosby and Bob Newhart albums over and over again had an influence on your personality. Maybe you were a big fan of

comedy on TV. Perhaps you developed a sense of humor to make friends or protect you from bullies. In any case, you would have had to find someone or something that would cause you to discover a knack for observing the absurd and developing a personality that could find humor in anything and everything.

There are exceptions to every rule and the above examples of early comedy development are certainly included. Whether you came from a good home or a broken home, rich or poor, "Leave It To Beaver" or "Divorce Court", your personality is susceptible to anxieties, phobias and compulsions that we all share. Feelings such as insecurity, shyness and inferiority could all have been covered up by humor during your formative years. These feelings can develop in anyone ... no matter which side of the tracks you were raised on. The fact that a sense of humor can develop from such negative feelings is a remarkable trait and one that many of the best stand-up comics in the business share.

It should be added that when we encourage finding humor in anything and not taking life seriously, we are not suggesting that kids should start goofing off! Some younger readers who may still be in school might take this as their ticket to forget about education and go strait onto the Carson show. Forget it gang ... it just doesn't work that way. Most comics are extremely well read and educated. After all, if you're going to make fun of something, you've got to know what you're talking about. Not taking life seriously means simply laughing at the world around you, not abandoning it. Don't forget that the most important thing to not take seriously is yourself. If you can't laugh at yourself, you'll have definite problems in comedy ... and in life!

Because there are not many ten-year-old stand-up comics, it's easy to prove that the decision to enter stand-up comes at a much later stage in life. There are, of course, numerous reasons for wanting to get into this business. The reasons range from the desires of fame and fortune to a simple attraction for making people happy. The important question to ask yourself when you begin to consider being a comic is what are YOUR reasons for getting into stand-up? What are your goals? Let's sort them out and take a look.

It's an established fact that everyone would enjoy expanding their fabled fifteen minutes of fame into a glamorous show business career. Everyone would love to be a star. However, if your sole reason for getting into comedy is to be famous, that's simply not enough. It takes years to get to a level where you MIGHT become famous and you would surely burn out long before that. If you're thinking about a comedy career to get rich quick or as an alternative to the lottery, forget it. Ask most working comics about the money they made when they began their careers and you'll probably get the biggest laugh of your stand-up life! NO ONE makes big money at the beginning stages of a comedy career, and those stages can run over a period of years.

So what's the deal? Why would anyone waste their time doing comedy? Good question. Amazingly, there are decent answers! If you enjoy entertaining people, if you enjoy making people laugh, if you enjoy the rush of being in front of 200 people and living on the edge, and if you enjoy being creative, writing consistently and working hard, then you just may be qualified to give comedy a chance. Here's what comedy will give you.

The ups and downs of show business careers have been well documented. It's no secret that it's a life of highs and lows. In comedy, the highs can be extremely high and the lows very low. The goals that you set out to meet when you entered comedy will make or break you in this period. If your goal was simply to make money and be famous, you'll never make it through the lows. You'll feel hurt and frustrated with every non-laughing audience member, every heckler, and each moment of desperation on stage. However, if you set aside attainable goals such as simply having the chance to be on stage and entertain ... getting a charge out of each laugh you get ... you'll find it much easier to make it through the rough times. If you have a bad set, you'll be anxious to get another crack at them next time. If your goal was to express your creativity, you'll use your time off stage to improve your material. With these simpler goals in mind, you will enjoy your "early years" much more and your odds of making it to riches and fame will improve.

Ahhh yes ... riches and fame. We know that these alone are not strong enough goals to get into comedy. Yes, we know we need to have a real love for the art of stand-up, but folks, let's not kid ourselves. Even if you set modest goals and are willing to be patient while waiting for success, everyone ultimately wants to make it big in the biz. While this is an enjoyable high in the comedy world, there are simpler and more reachable sparks of enjoyment along the way. For example, there are few greater feelings in the world than standing on stage and causing 200 strangers to laugh! The adrenaline flows strong when you're doing great on stage! There's also the joy of writing a great new joke or routine that works well on stage. Every successful bit that's added to your act proves you're growing as a comic.

As you continue through your comedy career, you will experience satisfaction with every advance you make up the levels of success ... "The Comedy Ladder." Some of these milestones include your first successful open-mike performance, your first one-nighter bookings and your first week-long bookings as an MC or opening act. From there, you can advance to the middle act slot and, if you continue developing your talent, onto headliner positions around the country. Further steps up the Comedy Ladder include opening shows for big name acts, auditioning for film and TV roles and performing stand-up on TV shows like "The Tonight Show."

But always remember that the thrill of reaching your first TV shot is the same in intensity as the thrill of having that first successful open mike set. The process just repeats itself as you stride towards your next rung on "The Comedy Ladder." If you pace yourself well and keep goals within your reach (not wishing to go directly from open mikes to the Oscars), then you'll do fine ... and keep your sanity too.

How long can this process take? Well all we can say is the classic line "don't quit your day job yet." Yes it takes years, even decades in some cases to reach the top, if you make the top at all. No matter what you read, there is no such thing as an "overnight success." True, some people seem to pop out of nowhere ... Dana Carvey, Jay Leno, Garry Shandling ... but these comics, like all of their peers, have years of comedy under their belt. Like any other career, you have to pay your dues before becoming a success. You'll gain knowledge and experience everytime you step on stage, and the more stage time you get, the quicker the road to success you'll have.

Finally, remember that comedy is a job. Sure it looks fun ... and it is, but there are still the usual elements associated with any job that apply to doing stand-up comedy. You're a worker. You get paid to work. You work for yourself, but the guy who pays you is the boss. There are some inside politics. There are commitments to make. There are sacrifices (often human). As far as a job goes, stand-up is sometimes no different from doing anything else. It's work!

Sacrifices? Did you say sacrifices? Did you say human sacrifices??? Yes and you should know this right off the bat. To make it in this business, you have to commit yourself to making yourself available for work anytime you can. Sometimes this is hard on the people that are closest to you. Wives/husbands/girlfriends/boyfriends are often the unwilling victims of a comedy career. You'll often be away from home at night for weeks at a time. Surely, this is tough on any relationship and you'll need an incredibly strong and supportive wife/husband/girlfriend/boyfriend to stick it out with you.

Keeping the day job is a financial necessity in staying in the biz for the first two to three years. Your pay, if anything, will be very little at first. You'll need that day job to cover your bills like anyone else and unfortunately, very few club owners will pay much for someone with no comedy experience. File this under "Paying Your Dues".

But people do make it in comedy and you can too if you have talent, set the right goals and are a tough-nut emotionally to hack it. If you are dedicated and believe in yourself, and believe you can be funny, then comedy could be your future.

You've got to be talented. You've got to be patient. You've got to be crazy! If you are, read on.

Chapter Two:
The Audience Monster

Deciding to BECOME a stand-up comic is easy. BEING a stand-up comic is the rough part. What's the dif? Just like anything else in life, actions always speak louder than words. Up to this point, you've had it easy telling people how funny you are. It's been a breeze to brag about someday becoming a big-time comedy star. Now it's time to show what you can do. It's time to start getting ready to meet your first audience.

Let's take a look at that audience. They sure look a lot different from your family and friends. For the first part, you don't even KNOW these people. These are veritable STRANGERS! Look at that front row. Six people within spitting distance! Two couples look like they're OK. They have their arms around each other and they're holding hands. Gee that's nice. Just some nice civilized patrons out to see some mid-week comedy. They'll be pushovers. You won't have any trouble making them laugh. You shouldn't have any trouble .... *whoops!* The waitress is bringing five rounds of Long Island Ice Teas to their tables. These bums will have to be carried out! *Oh no!!* Now the women are starting to chew tobacco and do bad animal impressions. The guys are impressing each other by farting. They're screaming incoherently at the top of their lungs! Oh look ... there's the manager. He'll shut them up. He'll probably kick them out. *OH MY GOD!!!* They're the manager's friends and he's bought them another round of drinks!!! You're just starting to realize that soon you've got to get out on that stage and make them laugh! Good luck just getting their attention!

The rest of the audience is starting to take the front row's lead and is becoming increasingly rowdy! Just then, you remember seeing all of those Harleys in the parking lot! Then you spot the sea of leather-clad, tequilla guzzling Hells Angels in the middle of the room! They're wearing eye patches and spitting on the floor. And that's the women! *Oh No!* Some seven-foot, 300 pound biker is standing up and screaming "WHERE'S THE #@*$ING COMEDIAN!" Now EVERYONE is yelling!

Surely, this is as bad as it gets! You ask yourself what could possibly top this! Then it happens. A bus load of fraternity brothers pulls up for a bachelor party! They've been nice enough to bring along their own kegs of beer which are being fed intravenously into their bloodstreams. They've decided to entertain the rest of the audience with a medley of obnoxious fraternity songs! *Oh great!* They're setting the groom on fire! You've never been to a bachelor party like this.

Gee. What a coincidence! The bikers happen to be old fraternity brothers themselves! Unfortunately, they're from a different fraternity. Now the two frats are yelling at each other. You begin to think "Isn't this how World War I started." Just as they start to come to blows, the girls from the front row begin to take off their clothes because their dates have bets going on who has the bigger boobs. At least this stops the fight. The bikers and the frats whoop and holler at a decibel range the Concord would be proud of. You notice the lights are going down. Hey ..... there's the MC. He's on stage trying to get the crowd's attention. He's going to bring you on .... *OH NO!!!* Someone shot the MC!!! GREAT! Now you hear your name over the PA from the back of the room. Your entire life has lead up to this moment! You're on!

Gee, it's too bad your Aunt Jim and Uncle Martha couldn't

make it to your first show. You are now experiencing your first law in comedy. YOU CAN'T PICK AND CHOOSE YOUR AUDIENCE! It would be great if there were IQ minimums at comedy clubs, but unfortunately this is not the case. You have to be ready for any kind of audience.

Therefore, when you're getting started in comedy, keep in mind who you're presenting your material to. These people are NOT your friends. They are NOT your family. They are called an AUDIENCE and they're made up of anybody and everybody. You can't expect them to know you or anything about you. These people don't know that you're funny. It's your job to prove you are. Believe us, these people will not take your word that you're a gifted comic, and they might get a bit nasty if they don't think you are! So with this in mind, let's go over some basic points on how to battle the Audience Monster!

Do you have any previous public speaking experience? Have you been up in front of crowds before? We're not even talking about a comedy club crowd here. Did you study speech in school? Were you a cheerleader? If you have spent any previous time standing alone in front of a mass group of people, you can draw from the experience and use it to your advantage. Overcoming fear is a major hurdle in doing stand-up. If the audience senses that you're uncomfortable being in front of them, you'll have a very tough time. The Audience Monster <u>can</u> smell fear. Your primary objective is to appear calm and totally

19

in control of yourself at all times while on stage. You must be prepared to overcome "flop sweat," that unique anxiety where you whittle down to a puddle of goop as you discover they're not laughing.

Nerves are a natural phenomenon in all of us. We really couldn't live without them. It's the body's process of preparing you for some important event. Nerves and fear can be related at times, but not necessarily always. It's possible to be a little nervous without being afraid. In fact, being nervous before a performance can be good! It gives you adrenalin and pushes you out onto the stage. Even performers at the very height of their careers have an inkling of nervousness before meeting an audience. It's purely natural. If you're nervous about going on stage, congratulations! You've got something in common with many successful performers.

If you're scared, that's a different story. Fear is what will keep you from doing comedy. Fear is what will spread self-doubt through your mind and have you bombing in your brain before you step out on stage. If your fears become exaggerated, voila! You're a wreck! You must learn to control any fear you have of the Audience Monster and hopefully eliminate it.

No one can teach you not to fear something. It's your own decision. You have to develop overcoming fear in your own time. There are some tips we can pass along to help though. If you have the previous public speech or performance experience we talked about earlier, you can certainly apply it to doing comedy. Let's face it! An audience is an audience whether you're in front of a comedy crowd or a church congregation. You're still in front of people - STRANGERS who don't know a thing about you. If you've won crowds full of strangers over before, you can win them over again...this time in comedy clubs!

If you don't have any of this experience, don't give up hope. You can still develop a method of dealing with your fear. In this audience versus performer game, keep in mind that the audience is really not some 600 pound, sharp clawed monster. They are just 200 or so fellow humans just like you. There is no reason why you should have trouble communicating with them. They share the same life experiences that you do. The audience knows what it takes to get up in front of people. They'd probably admit that they couldn't do it. Just by the fact that you're going to get up there in front of them commands their initial respect. Of course, this respect won't last through twenty to forty minutes of comedy, but it's a good start.

If you do have a fear about facing the Audience Monster, try to relax! Don't psych yourself out by assuming that the audience will initially know you're fearful of them. They're going to look at you as a professional performer ... someone who is not normally afraid to be in front of people. Try to imagine the audience as 200 of your closest friends. Plan to concentrate on looking calm, comfortable and together as much as possible when you appear on stage.

Comic Interview: Julia Duffy

How long have you been in comedy?
    2 years.
What comics influenced you?
    Carol Burnett, Joan Rivers, Lily Tomlin
Any advice for a new comic?
    Be persistant. Prepare to have a huge phone bill.
How has comedy benefited you?
    It took me out of the corporate world, which I think is a
    very sick environment.
What makes you a funny person?
    Being raised in Texas with cattle and severe heat. Also,
    knowing that if I'm not funny, I'll have to go back to the
    corporate world - sort of a "Russian Front" way of brainwashing
    myself.
What is the future of comedy?
    Hopefully, many more forums to work in. I hope comedy will
    stay as strong as it is because I have faith that people enjoy a
    good time and laughter.

A good trick when performing to a live audience is to look over their heads. Let's set up a stage situation in a typical comedy club. You'll be performing on a platform that is perhaps twenty feet by ten feet. There will be a microphone stand, a microphone and a stool. Over the heads of the 200 or so audience members will be several bright, glaring stage lights. When these lights are hitting you directly in the eye, as they will when you're performing, you'll be lucky to make out the first ten people in the room ... let alone the other 190. As the stage is possibly two to three feet higher than the audience's level, you'll find yourself looking directly into the stage lights and between them. Keep your focus on this area. Don't look down at the front row if you're afraid. Eye contact can be dangerous if you don't know how to handle it. You may discover someone's not laughing! Boy can THIS screw you up. If a comedy club is set up properly, the majority of the audience's perspective will show you looking directly at them. You on the other hand will see nothing but light and shadows under the stage lights. Light and shadows are nothing to be afraid of when performing comedy.

As you continue through a comedy performance, the Audience Monster can grow increasingly aware of any fears you might have. To combat this, plan to never fidgit on stage. Don't stand with your hands in your pockets. Take a breath here and there. Don't talk fast. Slow down. Relax. Never give the audience a clue that you've just ruined two weeks of perfect constipation right on stage.

As hard as it may seem to understand, remember that the audience is on your side. Put yourself in their place. They've stood in line. They've paid their money. Now they want to be entertained. So, more often than not, the audience will be very willing and intent on listening to what you have to say. These people actually will WANT YOU TO SUCCEED! For the most part, they really want you to do well. That's their payoff for coming to see the show. You can use this knowledge to gain some amount of self-confidence. While it's true that no two audiences are alike, and some will certainly be similar in spirit to the crowd we described earlier in this chapter, you should believe deep down in your comedy soul that each audience is pulling for you. They don't want, or expect you to be afraid of them.

Perhaps now you understand how to handle the Audience Monster a bit better. Maybe with this knowledge, you'll realize that your fear was exaggerated. The next battle is the fear of yourself ... you as a comedian. OK, sure, these are wonderful people in the audience. They're not aware that you're fearful of them. They've given you initial respect as a legitimate performer and they want you to do well. It sounds like they're fine. What about you?

Building self-confidence into a comedian is sometimes like trying to fit a square peg into a round hole. Many top comics who've spent years headlining clubs, appearing on TV and in films are still fighting a continuing battle for self-confidence to this day. Every new joke is scrutinized and many times they out and out ask audiences if a new bit is funny. They question if they're making the right career moves .... appearing on the right shows, having the right managers and agents. The bottom line is, there are few sure things for anyone in this business. As a beginning comic, however, this level of self-doubt should be the least of your problems. You have more basic things to work out first.

Quality, well written comedy material is your best possible weapon in your war against self-doubt and the Audience Monster. As much as you've heard from your family and friends about how funny you are, now you're out on your own and you have to prove it. You've got to build comedy material and develop a comedy *"set"* that you can professionally present to these "wonderful" people in the audience.

This is the point where self-confidence must be built. You might discover yourself asking the same questions over and over. Is my material funny? Will I forget something on stage? Will I get laughs?

Ultimately, you'll have to get up on a comedy stage to find the answers to these questions. Likewise, the only way to insure that the answers are in your favor is to develop quality comedy material.

Creating Material

Before attempting to write material, take an introspective look at yourself and discover what it is inside of you that makes you funny. Why are you the comic and others aren't? Are you funny in a physical, knock-about way? Do you have a unique thought process that twists logic for comedic effect? What elements of your personality do you feel others find humorous? Now, think about which comics you enjoy and why they are funny to you. Try to pick up the subtleties of timing and expression with which they successfully communicate with their audiences. Your goal here is not to become a carbon-copy of your favorite performer, but to build your own unique "*comic stage persona.*" This will be your stage character ... your attitude ... the image that the audience will see of you as a performer. By combining the influences of comics who make you laugh with the traits of your own personality that hopefully make you entertaining to others, your comic stage persona will begin to evolve. This is a long on-going process, the results of which could very well take years of performances to perfect. No doubt it will change many times during your comedy career. Your immediate goal as a beginning comic is to create an initial stage persona that you believe will get laughs and still be somewhat original ... somehow different from everybody else. It might not remotely resemble the performer that you'll eventually become, but it'll be enough to get you on stage for your first performance.

With an initial stage persona in mind, it's time to apply comedy material to it to see what fits. Material doesn't magically appear. Unlike what you may have heard or imagined, performers at the comedy club level do not make it a regular practice to buy material. It must be written and developed solely by each comic!

Sources for material are infinite and really not hard to find. Being a comedian after all is much like being a reporter. It's all there. You just have to find the subjects and present them in your own unique way. Day to day living experiences are the easiest and ones that the audience will have little difficulty in relating to. For example, activities such as driving, taking care of kids, being kids, flying, TV, and the battle of the sexes are universal topics and ones frequently visited by comics. Through the tint of your own personality and comedy persona, it's your job as a comic to look at these subjects and create humor ... observations that come from your own special comic world. With these observations in mind, you'll need to formulate them into comedy material, i.e. "Jokes", that can be consumed by an audience.

Though we're all familar with its basic format, it's important to take time to consider how a joke works. Comedy is based, among other things, on misdirection, the unexpected, the exaggerated and the absurd. To establish the foundation of a gag, a "*set up*" is necessary. This element introduces the audience to the direction your joke is taking. It should be clear and concise to lay the right groundwork for what's coming next. At the proper time, a "*punch line*" is added, steering the audience to an unexpected area causing laughter. Elements of exaggeration and absurdity further challenge the crowd's logic and result in good comedy. Naturally, these are very basic illustrations. Since comedy writing is an art form and by its very nature a creative process, there are unlimited variations to these examples. You are only limited by your imagination!

Try to imagine performing as you write. When creating material, consider how you'll communicate the joke to the audience. Correct timing and phrasing are key elements of good comedy and certainly among the top rules of the trade. When writing a gag, never say too much or too little. Find the minimum amount of words or actions necessary to best convey the set-up of the joke to the audience. The punch line should be delivered with equal directness. If you go too long setting up a bit, the joke will be anticlimatic. If you go too short, no one will know what the hell you're talking about. If you over-perform the punch line too much, the joke will die. If you don't punch the punch line enough, it will go right over their heads.

Your comic stage persona has a built-in style that will set the standards for what is "too much" and "too little" in writing bits. You must determine the proper phrasing for each gag by applying it to your stage character. Is it believable? Would this stage character communicate this way? Sometimes the addition or deletion of a sentence can improve a joke. Sometimes a single word can make a difference. It can be a certain inflection in your voice over a line or a different accent on one word. Any number of variables can be employed to tell one joke any number of ways, however, the only proper way to tell it is the way that gets the biggest laugh!

Comedy is not just words. When working out material, consider what body language you can use to add a big push for a joke. Discover the best physical way to communicate your material, either in an aggressive or subtle manner. Be expressive with your arms, hands, legs, walk, body position and facial looks. Let your body show that you're confident in your material. Vocally, plan to throw your voice to the entire crowd. Make sure the person in the last row will hear you. Let them know at least YOU enjoy these bits. However, when on stage, never laugh at your own material. Have fun and be happy, but laughing at your own jokes is unimpressive and annoying.

Sometimes when writing material, a single joke can lead to a second joke. This second joke is called a *tag*. The laughs generated by this tag can often be bigger than the original joke as you build audience response from one joke to the next. Tag jokes are the gags great routines are made of. A prime example of the tag joke pattern is Abbott and Costello's classic "Who's On First" baseball bit. Sure it's funny the first time Lou is fooled by "Who" playing first base. As it stands alone, it's a funny gag. But what made the routine infamous was the repetition of the same gag over and over and "tagging" it with new business at every turn. The danger of course is over-doing a good joke. However, if the bit is strong enough, it's possible to get a lot of mileage out of a single bit with the use of tags.

Make writing an enjoyable experience. The more writing you do, the sharper your material will become. Try to challenge yourself to find new subjects to do bits on. Keep on a constant watch for a new gag by carrying a scratchpad around to record spur of the moment ideas. If you see something with potential, write it down immediately. Later on, you can try to format it into a usable joke. Try not to let a day go by without thinking of some sort of possible gag. Keep your comedy material in notebooks for easy review. Concentrate on just writing single, quality jokes for the time being. Our next chapter will discuss building them into comedy sets.

Chapter Three
"50 Minutes??? Now THAT'S Funny!

How could any job be THIS EASY! You've been writing like crazy. You've written every day. You must have three notebooks full of material. Funny ideas are popping into your head at a regular rate. You might even be thinking that you have too much material! You wonder if Jay Leno might be interested in buying some of your surplus gags. Oh yeah ... you'd only give him the "B Stuff".

Wait a minute gang! Let's not lose our heads here. Hey it's great you're writing fluently. Writing EVERYTHING down genuinely helps. But try to realize that EVERYTHING you've written couldn't possibly be funny. Furthermore, even though you've packed three notebooks, ask yourself how much stage time your material will give you. You say you probably have 40 or 50 minutes in material? Think again!

We are familiar with the increments of time. Sixty seconds equal one minute. Sixty minutes equal one hour. Twenty-four hours equal one day. Etc. Somehow, stage time transcends all we have learned about traditional time keeping. The laws of stage time are completely out of whack with the physical laws of normal timekeeping. For some, being in front of 200 people can cause twenty minutes to seem like the blink of an eye. For others, twenty minutes can become an eternity.

When new comedians approach us and brag that they have 50 minutes of "great material," we naturally assume they MIGHT have five. This may sound unfair and non-supportive, but past experience with so-called "comic geniuses" forces us to instill a little piece of cold, hard reality into their lofty claims. We also know that the fledgling comic, who is aware of his or her limitations and lack of experience in gaging their material and stage time, will have a much better chance of making it in the long run.

The key to building that first set for your first audience is editing yourself. Let's assume that you've written those three note-books of material. Take our word for it, there might be some good stuff in there. There may even be some GREAT stuff in there. Ahhh, but huddled up in between the good stuff and the great stuff, you'll find just "stuff." This stuff is made up of gags that just aren't going anywhere. This material may have seemed hilarious at the time you wrote it down, but it just doesn't appear to play well now. How do you know for certain that a joke is funny? Talented veteran comics seem to know instinctively. Others have to rely on the opinions of audiences. Well, you're just getting started and you haven't met your first audience yet, so you're stuck.

Well, not really. Remember what the "Audience Monster" is made up of? That's right. 200 PEOPLE. Do you know any people? Of course you do. So don't hesitate to ask your friends and family what they think. Perhaps they'll be honest with you and give you constructive criticism on your material. Please take their advice with a grain of salt though. Remember you're playing on a home field advantage here. But their reactions can provide useful information.

Look at each joke objectively yourself. Can you deliver it in a way that the audience will easily relate to it? Do you have to go through miles and miles of set up before you get to the punchline? Is the punchline strong enough to overcome the miles and miles of set-up? Does any of this material sound dated to you? Are these bits too similar to another comic's material? Is the entire premise of the joke too obscure for the general audience? Ask yourself questions like

29

these when analyzing your comedy.

As you answer the questions, be prepared to throw some gags out. Set up your own standards for your material. Don't try to convince yourself that a joke is funny when you know it's not. Remember that all jokes are not created equal. Throw out the stinkers. You'll replace them with something better.

In among all of your material will be gags that "just seem OK." They're not terrific, but they might have potential for laughs. Somewhere inside there's a joke just screaming to get out, but as it reads right now, it falls flat. Keep these puppies and work with them a little. Perhaps they need a different set up or maybe the timing is off in your delivery. You might be able to improve a mediocre gag and make it a useful part of your material. Tell the joke over and over to yourself until you've brought the bit to its best possible presentation.

Be honest when editing and critiquing your material. You can be assured that if you're not, the audience will be. If it's not funny, they'll be happy to let you know.

Part of this editing process relates to our previous topic of your comic stage persona. Do these jokes fit in with your personal style? Is this the type of comedy that seems natural for you to perform? At this point, the issue of "clean or dirty" material appears. When editing yourself, you'll eventually face a blue or dirty joke. It could be the funniest joke in all three of your notebooks. You could probably tell it to your friends .... maybe a brother ..... maybe a sister ..... but could you tell it to your mom? How about your Aunt Jim and Uncle Martha? You've met a comedy dilemma. The problem is that all of your friends, brothers, sisters AND your parents, aunts and uncles are part of your audience. The comedy crowd is made up of all types of people similar to your friends and relatives. Ask yourself if your personal style will allow you to tell a blue joke to every 50 year old lady in the audience. If you can't see yourself doing it, throw it out no matter how good the laugh is.

We realize that the comedy industry is filled with entertainers that work dirty. Many of them are working the comedy club circuit and getting good money. Few of them will ever leave the comedy club circuit. It is our opinion that relying on a dirty act will hold you back from being a quality comedian. Limiting yourself to blue material will in turn limit your marketability in a comedy career. Blue comics should not be confused with comedians that occasionally dip into blue material. These entertainers have the flexibility to work clean or dirty. They have not limited themselves to continually recycling the same dirty jokes. This act would still stand on its own without the blue material and work well to any crowd.

Not performing blue material doesn't necessarily mean not discussing adult topics. Your typical comedy audience is not made up of people who couldn't make it to Miss Nancy's Romper Room taping. For the most part, these are adults, college age or better, who are more than likely situated in a comedy club drinking alcoholic beverages. When we suggest to stay away from blue material, we're not talking about limiting yourself to knock-knock jokes. Controversial adult topics are fine to discuss. It's open season on anything from politics to sex. The art of stand-up comedy and the difference between a blue comic and a clean comic is how the material is handled. For example, a blue comic will discuss sex very graphically, possibly even with visual aids. This could be offensive to even the most liberal of audience members. The clean comic can perform the same type of material, possibly even the same joke and get away with it using inuendo. We know what they're talking about. We get the joke. We just don't need a lesson in sexual body parts and graphic expressions of sexual intercourse to get the point. You may find it easier to say the joke in a blue fashion and even get a healthy laugh, but the laugh can be greater if you perform it clean without embarrassing the audience.

Another pitfall frequently visited by new comics is the "FuckShitDickTit" syndrome. These words are often heard in comedy sets. They have become such a part of the popular vernacular that you can't go through a day without hearing them on the inside or outside of a comedy club. Just as we suggested to stay away from blue material when editing yourself, we also recommend being careful not to get into this bad habit. If you are a slave to the FuckShit DickTit syndrome, you are limiting your marketability just like the blue comic. It is not our intention to try to keep you from using Fuck-ShitDickTit or words like them in your act. The issue here is making sure you don't rely on them, much like the blue comic must rely on dirty material for their laughs.

Many comics will add a four-letter word to a punchline for a bigger laugh. For example, the reaction seems to be bigger if you change "So I bit him" to "So I *fuckin'* bit him." Same joke. Bigger laugh. Why? The joke becomes the word "fuckin." The original premise of the gag is swallowed up by a four-letter word. If the joke can't work without the extra word, maybe the joke isn't funny to begin with. Some comics make careers out of performing mediocre material and adding their FuckShitDickTits in. They end up doing marginally well, but they have many harsh realities to face for cheapening their act. First of all, there are a billion comics working today. There are only so many clubs. There are fewer breaks to TV and beyond. With an unlimited talent-pool to choose from, TV producers don't look at the words FuckShitDickTit. They look at the jokes. If the joke is there, the producer will see it. If the joke is only FuckShitDickTit, the producer will see that too. This FuckShitDickTit comic's chance of success will be slim.

Look what happened to your three notebooks worth of mate-

rial! You're down to about one and a half! Well, that's still not too bad! Now your challenge is to take your material and build a "comedy set" out of it. Because you haven't performed professionally yet, you have no real idea of how long it takes to deliver your material. The obvious step is to time it. Grab a watch and your material. Run through your gags, one right after the other, and time yourself. Don't give yourself thirty seconds of laughs between each joke. Most comics are happy with five and you may not get any. Deliver each joke in a natural rhythm just as if you were on stage. When you've completed this, you'll have an idea of the minimum stage time needed to perform all of your material. Our guess is you might have fifteen minutes total .... that's all of the good stuff, the great stuff and the questionable stuff. Everything.

Your first comedy performance will undoubtedly be at one of comedy's most traditional events ..... *The Open Mike Night*. The format of a comedy club open mike is generally a parade of comics, one right after the other, performing five to ten minute sets. Comics of all levels of experience may perform on any given night. The "Robin Williams, Richard Pryor" guys may drop in to work on new material. There may be national club headliners showcasing for the club's owners. Then there will be thirty people like yourself waiting to take their first steps into comedy.

Comic Interview: **Ron Reid**

How long have you been in comedy?
>8 years

What comics influenced you?
>Steve Landesberg, Bob Newhart, David Steinberg, David Letterman

Any advice for a new comic?
>Be original! Don't sacrifice long-term goals for "getting over." Contrary to popular opinion, comedy is art. That means, creating something that never existed before.

What makes you a funny person?
>With a face like this?

How has comedy benefited you?
>It's allowed me an outlet for creativity that's immensely satisfying ... and lets me sleep late.

What is the future of comedy?
>Comedy has always been with us. Humor is our way of dealing with great stress and taboos, and provides us with a safe outlet for the reduction of anxiety. Comedy will always be with us, although many comics will eventually go to graduate school. The truly talented and committed performers will become part of the national talent pool of actors and entertainers. The rest will become agents or drive taxis.

Once you've gotten the green light to perform at an open mike, find out the format of the show. Let's assume the format is a ten minute set. Now your job is to structure your material into ten minutes of rip-roaring comedy. Everyone has seen comics perform on TV shows. They have a prepared act that flows from subject to subject. From the "Good Evening Ladies and Gentlemen" to the "Thank You and Good Night," it sounds natural and professional. Actually it's just a string of different gags arranged in a strategical order, but the entire set appears consistent in content throughout. You can arrange your material into a comedy set for a similar result by following several simple guidelines.

Out of the fifteen minutes of material you have, you're obviously going to have to lose five to fit in your ten minute set. List all of your jokes on a sheet of paper. It's not necessary to write out the entire gag. Perhaps, just the premise and the punchline or a single catch word that will remind you of the joke. Now you can see all the subject matter that you'll cover in your set. To eliminate the five minutes, take out the jokes that are questionable first. Don't throw them away yet. They might be able to be salvaged at a later time.

Now group the remaining jokes together into subjects. For example, driving jokes, dog and cat jokes, TV jokes, whatever. Under the different categories, give each joke a grade as to its quality. "A," "B," "C" and so on down the line. If you still need to cut more time to make your set run ten minutes, edit out the weaker graded material. The remaining jokes will comprise your comedy set.

Take a look at all of the categories now. Try to arrange the jokes in a logical order so that when they're presented in succession they'll make sense. This will develop the raw material into consistant "*routines*." Now give a grade to each routine based on its overall quality strength. Maybe your driving routine has two or three Great Jokes, but five so-so jokes. Give it a "C." Look at the jokes in the TV bit. They're all killer. This is the "A" stuff. Your dog and cat gags are just OK, so give the routine a "D." You also have a pair of great lines about living with your parents. Give it a "B." Assign a different grade from the best to the worst on all of your routines. Now you can organize your set.

The traditional comedy set begins by acknowledging the audience. Plan to say some form of small-talk greeting to them such as "Good Evening" or "How are you folks doing tonight." It is a comedy law that the first fifteen seconds of your perfomance can be very important to your set. With this in mind, choose the grade "B" routine about your parents to open up. Maybe you can slide into your set by thanking them for giving you a ride over to the club tonight and then punch the routine's jokes. This enables you to casually begin your material in a natural manner. Since the routine was great enough to be graded second highest, you should get a good response from the crowd. Thus, in the first fifteen seconds of your planned routine, several important things should have already occured. By greeting the crowd, you've created an element of communication between you, the performer, and the audience. They've recognized that you're going to entertain them and they have given you the initial respect that will carry you over to the first joke. From this point on, it's up to you and your material. But hey! Don't worry! That first routine about your parents has two great jokes that will surely get big laughs. This will establish you as a funny person to the crowd. Therefore, in the first fifteen seconds of your planned set, you've told the audience that you're worthy of their respect and that you're funny to boot! This is a good start.

If sets were fifteen seconds long, you'd be a headliner. But that's not the case. Plan to follow up your opening lines with your third highest graded material ... the driving routine, which was graded "C." Figure out a way to gracefully get onto the subject of driving from the previous jokes about your parents. This is called a "*segue*". Segues are a masterful art and a prime component of a quality comedy set. The object is to keep the flow going and not to jump the audience around too much. Don't go from a joke about your parents into a driving routine that starts with "I got three speeding tickets last week." In this particular example, there is an easy way to segue. After your parents material, say "My dad's a rotten driver ... of course, I guess I'm not much better. I got three speeding tickets last week." By adding this simple line, you've successfully brought two unrelated subjects together into one continuing routine while the audience barely noticed the switch in material. This segue has added a smooth professional touch to your set.

Many comics segue by going to the audience with a question. In our example, a comic might go from material on parents to asking the audience if "anybody here hate getting traffic tickets?" Naturally, the audience will respond and be prepared for the driving gags. Although not as smooth as our first example, this segue regardless opens up a new subject successfully. Talking to the crowd in this manner also adds to your performer/audience communication level. During your set, you can go to the crowd many times with questions ... as long as their relevant to your act and have a meaningful purpose. However, there have been examples of comics who ask too many questions, which invites TOO MUCH participation on the crowd's part. This can lead to heckling and group discussions within the audience. When you go to the crowd, you must stay in control of the group at all times.

Continue arranging each routine in a logical order as well as designing smooth segues for each changing subject. Vary the quality of the bits as you build your set. Don't lump all of the lower graded material at the end. Mix the routines with the most potential in with the ones with the least.

One other strong punch to your stand-up set is a method called the *"Call Back."* It is a technique of recalling an earlier joke from an earlier routine later in the set. It can be used by repeating a certain punchline, a character or anything else the audience can relate to that they previously heard. A successful Call Back will not only punch the latter joke for a bigger laugh, but also help the audience recall the original gag and bring the entire comedy set full circle. As with any other method of creating comedy, Call Backs can be overused, however with the right balance, they can become a very effective addition to your set.

Plan to use your grade "A" material last. This will give you a rousing finale to your set and ensure getting off stage on a laugh. This is important. If you're a comic, there's nothing worse than saying goodnight to a non-laughing audience. "Always leave them laughing" is the old adage and it certainly applies here. Just as the first fifteen seconds were vital to the beginning of your set, your last fifteen seconds are equally important for a successful conclusion. The audience has an unfortunate habit of remembering you by your last fifteen seconds. Just as their initial judgment of you from the beginning of your set got you through your act, their final judgment

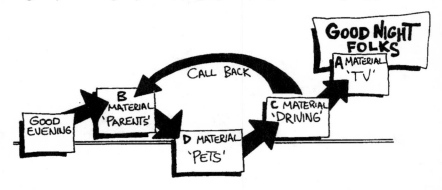

of you at the end will be their last sumation of your performance. The question is "Will They Remember You." If your closing fifteen

38

seconds are your best, there's a chance they will.

Once you've edited your material down to your best ten minute comedy set, it's recommended that you rehearse your act. With your material locked away in your memory, perform your set to yourself out loud in front of a mirror. Work each bit as if you were on stage in front of 200 people. Look for any improvements you can make in timing and delivery. Watch yourself perform in the mirror and see if any physical movements can be added to make your bits stronger. Keep in mind that this method offers a <u>limited</u> amount of insight and discovery into how well your set will be received by a comedy crowd and cannot equate to the vast knowledge and experience you'll gain from performing to a live audience. However, this rehearsal method will assist you in gaining familiarity with your material, help you become more comfortable with it and better prepare you for your audience.

When you feel you're ready, it's time to take your set to the world. It's time for the acid-test of comedy. It's time to try it in front of REAL PEOPLE!

It's time for an Open Mike.

Chapter Four:
That First Open Mike

Rod Serling could not have done a better job.

You've been writing for weeks. You've edited and polished your material into a nice tight ten minute set. You're sure of yourself. You've built some confidence. You've contacted a local comedy club in your area. You've been successful in getting a spot on an Open Mike Night. (Can you hear the "Twilight Zone" music beginning?) On your way to the club on that fateful night, you discover beads of sweat pouring down your face. Your stomach fights off that burrito you wolfed down for dinner. The radio station begins to play a three-hour Barry Manilow / Captain and Tennille Music Sweep. A sudden gust of wind blows through an open window and scatters all of your notes of material. As you try to organize your papers, you hit a parked car with the license plate "CLUB OWNER" on it. Suddenly you've realized that you're not in Kansas anymore. You've entered The Comedy Club Zone.

Let's hope your first night as a performer isn't as traumatic as this! Your first Open Mike might very well be a disaster. But it can also be a very rewarding experience.

The comedy club Open Mike Night was created to discover new talent and to give an opportunity to all to work on their routines before a live (hopefully) audience. As we stated in our last chapter, an open mike performance roster can feature talent from the total spectrum of experience. Newcomers may find themselves sharing the bill with national headliners. Although this might appear to be a pressure situation, quite the opposite is true. By design, open mikes are low pressure performances. (Do yourself a favor and don't invite all your friends and family to your *first* open mike. You don't need to add any pressure.)

The Open Mike audience can be as varied as the performers. Regular club customers mingle with new patrons who are taking advantage of the low or sometimes non-existant cover charge for the show. In our experience, we have found that these low admission charges may very well fill up the room on an off night, but they don't necessarily insure a top comedy audience. When something is given away at a low price or for free, it is generally not as appreciated as it normally would be. We found this often to be true with comedy shows. Audiences who have paid reduced admissions to a show tend to be rowdier and a little less patient. Drinking also appears to increase as the customers use the money they saved on the admission to buy extra rounds of alcohol. This doesn't necessarily make for a great crowd.

Besides this basically unstable audience base, other comics might invite friends to the show with the hope that they'll help with a partisan response to their set. Often these patrons will leave after they've seen their favorite act causing a high turnover of audience members throughout the evening. Chairs moving, ash trays being cleaned and tables being bussed are not terrific sounds to do comedy by. However you must remember that running any nightclub, including a comedy club is a business. The extra noise unfortunately is a necessary evil. If you can learn to deal with it, it can only improve your ability as a comic.

Some clubs have no choice but to seat the assembled multitude of comics in the audience with regular customers during an Open Mike. The hardest room to play to in comedy is a room full of other comedians. They're not necessarily rude and it's rare that they would vocally interfere with your act. They simply won't be great laughers! They've heard it all before. Instead of reacting to your material, they're more likely to be watching your style. They'll sum you up by audience response and the quality of your set. When they watch other comedians, comics often laugh at gags no one else laughs at. It could be a totally off-the-wall remark that goes right over the audience's head, or another comic's blooper that sets them off. There might be an inside joke involved. In most cases, the audience hasn't a clue as to what's so funny and why the other comics are breaking up. We suggest that you not be too concerned about making the other comics laugh. Your job is to entertain the audience.

When you arrive at the comedy club, introduce yourself to the person in charge, either the manager or owner. Even though you have no previous experience beforehand, attempt to act professional at all times. This is very important, especially when dealing with a club manager or owner. This person is your boss for the evening and should command your respect. Don't put on an air or attitude about yourself. As a beginning comic, stating over-confident expressions like "I'm gonna kill this crowd," "You should be headlining me" or "I didn't know your club was so smelly" will not endear you to the boss. Be friendly and businesslike. Make sure you've given yourself plenty of time to get to the show early. Club owners and managers like to have the comics on-hand long before the show begins. If they told you to be at the club a half-hour before the show starts, BE THERE AT THE CLUB A HALF-HOUR BEFORE THE SHOW STARTS. This is all a part of establishing good relations with a comedy club.

Open mike order slots are assigned in many different ways. At our clubs, we use a random card drawing method. Each comic pulls a card out of a hat as they arrive at the club. This card determines the slot they receive. Other clubs arrange the show in the order that the comics signed up ..... those that signed up early appear in the early part of the show and so on. Then again, some clubs simply use the manager or owner's discretion in establishing the order. He or she may put the stronger acts strategically in the latter part of the evening to keep the audience as long as possible.

Regardless of which method is used to establish an order, don't expect the manager to give you an exact time for your appearance. You should expect to be at the club the entire run of the evening's performance. Several factors can interfere with planning your scheduled time to hit the stage. First of all, even though the show is formated for ten minute sets, some comics might go long. This won't necessarily put them in good favor with the club; in fact, it shows a lack of respect for the club's operation and producer. There are numerous examples of those poor departed souls who go twenty minutes over without a single laugh. As far as the club is concerned, these people will not be seen again.

Just the opposite is also true. Comics may go short on their alloted time. This is usually a sign of inexperience, but gaining experience is what Open Mikes are all about. If a comic does half of his or her scheduled time, but at least gets some good laughs with quality original material, they will find encouragement from club managers and other comics.

To help control the length of sets and to assist the comics, most clubs install a hidden signal light which can be seen only by the performer on stage. Depending upon the club, this may be a one minute, five minute or whatever minute signal to the comic letting them know their stage time status. We prefer the five minute light. It allows the comics enough time to do their final routines and end their sets smoothly.

Many clubs in bigger cities invite unscheduled guests to perform during the evening. These "drop-in" acts can enter the club at a moment's notice and be added immediately to the schedule. They generally take the next available spot and are on stage as soon as possible. Few performers however have the necessary pull to disrupt an open mike schedule. Those that do are basically given free reign and can do sets as long as they wish. Often those comics who had the late scheduled slots will get "bumped" because of this and must be rescheduled for a later date. Those performers who had nice cozy mid-evening slots could end up doing their sets at the close of the night.

The bottom line ... there's no sure way of knowing when you'll be asked to perform, so be patient and available. It's in your best interest.

After you've made your introductions to the management and have been assigned your scheduled slot, have a seat in the area that has been set aside for the comedians. Try at all times to stay out of the club employees way as they go about their jobs preparing for the show. Introduce yourself to other comics. Be sociable. However, by all means try to keep modest to the other acts. Don't tell them how funny you are. They will likely tear you apart.

It is possible that the club will have a "*green room*," a place set aside as a special area for performers to relax and wait before they go on stage. Since all of the show's performers must use this area, make sure you show consideration to your fellow comics. Don't invite friends to sit in the green room with you. Clean the area up after yourself. Keep things respectfully quiet (sometimes sound carries to the stage). Remember always that a green room, no matter how much it looks like a rat hole, is a courtesy, and the courtesy you show in sharing it with other comics will help everyone out.

As the room fills up, you might want to take a good look at the crowd. Study some of the faces in the front row. These are the people you'll be facing tonight. Try to break down that "audience monster" fear as soon as possible by getting familiar with the people in the room.

Talk to the MC who'll be starting the show soon. Ask him where the signal light is and if he needs to know anything about you for an introduction. If he wants some info, don't load him up with your life story. Simply tell him where you're from and that this is your first time on stage. If he's a good MC, he'll give you a good introduction that will have the audience behind you at the start. The MC, after all, is also trying to put on a good show.

As the show begins, the MC will likely greet the group and do five or ten minutes up front. The MC has been chosen as an already established entertainer who can hold a crowd and keep the show going in a professional manner. Many times an MC is an old open mike alumni. The experience he gained by participating in numerous open mikes has brought him to this level. An MC's material must be good enough to carry a good portion of the show in the event that the acts are horrible. At least, the audience will see SOME good comedy during the evening. A quality MC will run the show at a fast pace. If there is a lull in the performance, possibly due to a comic who did poorly, the MC can do some material to bring the audience back in time for the next performer. Indeed, the MC holds a major responsibility for the overall success of the show.

Comic Interview: John Pate

How long have you been in comedy?
    12 years
What comics influenced you?
    Jackie Gleason, Jay Leno
Any advice for a new comic?
    Write your own material and keep it clean. You will work
    forever.
What makes you a funny person?
    The fact that I have remained a virgin for 31 years and
    counting.
How has comedy benefited you?
    I've been able to make a living at what I enjoy doing most.
    That's all I can ask for.
What is the future of comedy?
    I see eskimo comedy in the near future, after which jugglers
    will make a comeback.
Any additional comments?
    I never met a comic I didn't like. However, there are two
    that I don't consider comics.

It is a good idea to watch and learn from the MC. Working as an MC is one of the best ways to get stage time early on in your career. Watch how they handle the crowd. Learn how they keep the show exciting despite the possible mediocrity of the acts. Chances are, you will eventually find yourself at the MC position. It is great experience and usually some of your first paid work as a performer.

These open mikes are truly an excellent opportunity to watch other comics at work and learn from them. They may not be doing anything remotely similar to your style, but you can pick up the finer points of the craft. Look for methods of stage presence, delivery and timing and compare them with your own. These suggestions for observation in no way implies STEALING MATERIAL! Perhaps this is your first time watching other comics as a performer. Temptation might set in and you might feel the urge to directly steal material or another comic's gimmicks. The word here is DON'T. D-O-N-APOSTROPHE-T!!! Stealing material is the top taboo in comedy. There are those who've made careers out of it. Some have marginally become successful. All have lost the respect of fellow comics and the industry. If you think your routines aren't strong enough and you can't get by without ripping somebody off, do us all a favor and get out of the business. More and more comedy producers are refusing to hire comics who steal and their names pass swiftly around comedic circles. If you're trying to make a career out of stolen material, forget it.

Watch how the show is progressing. This is a luxury that is not afforded to the opening comics. Take notice on how good the crowd is (are they responding well, laughing heartily or sitting like bumps on a log). Look for the rowdy corners of the group (find the trouble spots and try to ignore them while on stage). Listen to the quality of the sound system. Check out the microphone positions. Check where the speaker systems are located. Listen for extra background noise such as blenders and bar staff. Get a feel for the "energy" of the room, the environment the audience is in. Use the knowledge of this energy when performing your set.

When the comic before you is introduced, make sure you're in the green room preparing to go on. Quickly run over your material. As a newcomer, you can never, Never, NEVER take notes out on stage with you. This is perhaps the most unprofessional thing a beginning comic can do. By now, we hope that you are familiar enough with your routines that you won't need them. Check your appearance. Are you dressed and groomed in a manner that fits your stage persona? Don't wear tattered T-shirts and cut-offs unless your stage character is a burnt-out surfer-dude. It always helps to look good for an audience. It shows respect for the crowd and establishes you in a non-verbal fashion that you're a true entertainer. If you look like you just walked off the street, that is the image the audience will pick up. Keep in mind that the audience's visual perception also has a great influence on their overall impression of you as a performer.

You're starting to feel a little nervous inside. As the comic before you dies a slow death and says good night, you hear the crowd applauding and the MC returning to the stage. You see the exiting comic return to the green room complaining about the audience. It really was all *their* fault wasn't it.

Going on stage doesn't have to be traumatic. Have a little faith in your material and ability. Tell yourself that you're funny and you're about to prove it to these people. At any rate, there's nothing that can be changed now. The audience is waiting for you. They won't go away. The MC is about to introduce you. You can't stop that now. You might as well make the best of this situation. Get out there and do the best that you can!

The MC gives the audience two minutes of good laughs, a needed release from the tension built by the struggling comic who just bombed. You're about to be introduced. Check your fly and jump up and down. Get your energy going. Listen for that introduction.

You're on!

From the second you hit the stage, let your body communicate all the energy necessary to establish your stage persona early. If your act is high energy, throw yourself onto the stage in an aggressive style. Show the crowd you mean business. If you're taking a more intellectual style, walk out in a manner that will tell the audience that you're comfortable with them and you're worthy of their respect. The bottom line is don't just lump up to the mike and give the impression that you'd rather be anywhere but here because you're scared to death. You're not giving a science report in the sixth grade. You're an entertainer. Make every move count. *Entertain!*

Just as your energy level has an influence on the audience, the audience's energy level also affects your performance. If the crowd is small, quiet and withdrawn, you might have to curb back your energy to suit them. If your jumping up and down and screaming your jokes out to fifteen people as if they were 300, you'll overkill your routines. Initially at least when dealing with small crowds, tone down your energy and let the fifteen or so audience members get a chance to catch up with you. Once you "lock in" with the group and start getting laughs, you can begin to bring the energy back up.

There are only two universal props in stand-up comedy. The microphone and mike stand. There are two basic ways to use the mike stand. Either let it hold the mike or don't. While this may seem trivial to you now, remember that the mike stand is the only thing standing between you and the audience. There is a certain unconscience message you give the crowd when you take the mike off that stand and place the stand behind you. You're taking away the only barrier between you and the audience. You are totally revealing yourself to the crowd. Many comics prefer to stand behind the mike stand throughout their entire set. This is fine too. Some use the rock star approach and simply drag the stand around all night. If you take the mike off, you can use the stand to your advantage. You can lean on it, play with it, hang a jacket on it, use it for sight gags or just let it sit behind you. Use the stand like you'd use any tool of the trade. Use it to add to your stage presence and let it become part of your stage persona.

The microphone of course is the main communication link between you and the audience. There are certain guidelines for proper mike use. First of all, remember that a microphone is a costly, integral part of the club's sound system. It might not look like much, but improper use of a mike can cause severe damage quickly. Dropping the mike, throwing it or banging it against unyielding surfaces won't do much good for this fragile tool. Like the stand, the mike can at times be used for sight gags. Just use common sense. Judge for yourself whether a $200.00 microphone is worth a small laugh from the front row.

Learn the proper way to hold the mike. Hold it approximately four to six inches away from your mouth. Don't "eat" the microphone. Don't have it too far away either. Make sure the audience can hear you well and understand what you're saying. Because you made a mental note by watching the other comics before you, you'll know the quality of the sound system and have some idea on how to hold the mike for the best communication with the audience. Don't forget the positions of the speakers off stage. Take care not to send feedback into the sound system by holding the microphone too close to the speakers. Naturally this will cause blood-curdling shrieks from the sound system upsetting you, the audience and the club personnel.

Comic Interview: Bob Worley

How long have you been in comedy?
 6 years
What comics influenced you?
 Bill Cosby, Steve Martin, my mom and dad and friends.
Any advice for a new comic?
 Write and perform as much as possible
What makes you a funny person?
 I see the humorous side of everything. There's a joke
 everywhere you look.
How has comedy benefited you?
 A way of staying out of a real job and doing what I love to do
 the most - perform and make people laugh.
What is the future of comedy?
 I wish I knew.
Any additional comments?
 I have always felt that comedy was an art form and that you
 should do what is funny to you and what you know about, and
 not what's "in" at the time.

Run through your material on stage as you rehearsed it. At this level of your experience, it's not recommended that you try adlibbing

51

in front of a live audience. Just get through this first set. Make sure you're being expressive with your body language. Use your arms and hands to support your voice. Remember to never look down and not to look directly at the crowd. Look over their heads. Look between the lights and through the crowd. Don't let the audience monster loose on your first comedy performance.

As you go through your routines, give a natural amount of time for each laugh. Establish an appropriate rhythm in your performance. LISTEN to the laughs of the audience and pace your delivery naturally to them ... much like you would in a one on one conversation. Don't count 1,2,3,4,5 between each and every joke. If there's no laugh, move right onto the next bit. If there's a healthy laugh, a long break might be in order. If it's just a chuckle, wait a second and then continue. Timing and pacing greatly come into play here. If this comes hard at first, don't worry. This can only be gradually developed through time ... stage time ... and lot's of it!

Move around the stage a little bit. Play to all corners of the room. Lighten up and have a little fun. Keep good expression in your voice and make sure everyone is hearing you. Don't overkill your per-formance. Don't turn your back to the crowd. Nag nag nag ... you get the hint.

If there's a point in your set where things aren't going too well, don't freak out. No matter how bad it gets, never acknowledge to the audience that a routine is bombing especially if you're a new comic. Sympathy doesn't work well in comedy rooms and you'll have a very difficult time getting the audience back. Naturally, if the crowd begins to break off into small discussion groups during a routine, you may want to go onto the next part of your set. Club owners would rather see a good five minutes from a newcomer than a terrible ten.

Remember to look for the signal light. When it comes on, prepare to shift into your closing material no matter where you are in your set. Be able and willing to edit yourself while on stage.

At the end of your set during the last laugh, thank the audience and tell them you hope they enjoy the rest of the show. Try to work your name into your closing patter as well. A good example is to say "Thank you folks. You've been a great crowd. I've been *so and so*. Enjoy the rest of the show." Return the mike to the mike stand and place it back at the center of the stage. Shake the MC's hand as you leave the stage (that is if your hand isn't sweaty as hell from this experience).

Whew! It's over. You've gotten through your first comedy performance. Some parts of your set went well. Some parts fell apart. Others need a little work. Analyze your set and make necessary adjustments. Ask the other comics for suggestions. Ask the club owner or manager for their opinions. They will be glad to give you advice on your set. These people see comedy every night and they're well versed in comedy through their experience. They may have some useful tips on tightening up your set.

Before you leave the comedy club that night, make sure you've found out when the next open mike night is. Make sure you're at it. Open mikes are golden opportunities. Unfortunately, there's no gold involved. These open mike gigs seldom pay anything. The rewards of open mike nights are performances. Performances which are not in front of a mirror. Not in front of your Aunt Jim and Uncle Martha. These are performances in front of real comedy club audiences. This is real life STAGE TIME, the only method of truly becoming a quality comic. The more stage time you can get early in your career, even at open mikes, the more valuable knowledge you'll gain about your comedic potential! You can't pay enough for the knowledge that a room full of 200 people will give you as they listen to your set.

Being a newcomer to the business, your enthusiasm is at its highest. Use this energy and enjoy just the charge of being on stage and learning your new craft. Sure there's room for improvement, but at this early point, you'll only start getting better. It takes TIME and your time has begun!

Chapter Five:
Making Open Mikes Count and YOU as an "MC"

Consider how lucky you are.

As we look ahead into the 1990's, the hottest entertainment phenonomen is Comedy. Comedy has broken out of movie and TV studios and into every nook and cranny of Anytown, USA. Comedy clubs are leading the charge of course, but comedy rooms are also springing up in hotels, bowling alleys and practically anyplace else that has a microphone. The beauty for you, the aspiring comic, is that there are now thousands of stages across the country for you to develop your act on. This wasn't always the case though. As little as ten years ago, there were only a handful of comedy rooms on the national circuit. Comics were extremely competitive for the limited amount of stage time available. Naturally, it was very difficult for new comics to work out their material.

Today however, it's a whole new ballgame. You should feel fortunate that you are starting your career in these times-o-plenty for new comedians. You've made the decision to enter stand-up. You've written your first set of comedy. You've met your comedy acid-test with your first open mike. You now must decide just how far you're going to commit yourself to this wacky business. There is a lot of opportunity for you, but you have to be willing to grab it.

As we recommended in our last chapter, make sure you make it a regular practice to do open mikes at your local comedy club. It's amazing, but some people actually believe that comics perform different material everytime they appear on stage. Performers like Robin Williams make their act look so spontaneous that some audience members find it difficult to realize that this is prepared material that has been performed before. These individuals believe that all comedians are saying their jokes for the very first time. This could not be further from the truth. You'll want to keep working with your existing material ... using it over and over for each set.

With each performance and each audience, measure the response to your material. Once you've worked with your original material a few times, start playing around with it a bit. Edit routines out that don't work very well and replace them with ones that improve your set. Continue writing every day and begin to try something new each time you work an open mike. Experiment and have fun, but remember not to push the patience of the audience too much. If their response to a bit continues to be minimal, and you've exhausted every possible method of trying to make it funny, get rid of it.

It is a very good idea to tape every set you do. Buy yourself one of those hand-held cassette recorders. No you're not going to be taping the live album. This is simply a very popular method used by many comics for analyzing their performances. Tape a set sometime and listen to yourself perform. You'll be amazed at how differently you sound compared to how you think you sound. There's lots to learn too! Are you speaking clear enough? Are you talking too fast? Are you accenting the right words? Is your delivery correct? Can anything be improved? Compare audience response from two different perform- ances. If the laughs were bigger in one show over the other, find out why! It's very possible that some slight nuance in your presentation "pushed" the joke for a bigger laugh. These discoveries will vastly improve your timing and delivery.

Many clubs now have video tape capability. This has become a major benefit for comedians. Now you can watch your performance as the audience actually sees you. Watch your body language and movement and see if you're communicating properly to the audience. Make adjustments where necessary. Video has additional benefits which we will discuss later.

Another benefit of taping your performance is the possibility of salvaging ad-lib bits that appear out of nowhere while you're doing your set. As you continue doing comedy and become more comfort- able with the comedy stage, there will be moments when a quick one- liner will appear out of nowhere. Many times, the "rush" from being on stage produces some of a comedian's most creative moments. It could be a quick response to the crowd. It could be a tag line to an existing routine that you hadn't thought of. Whatever it is, you have it on tape. If it got a good response on stage, you'll be able to go back to a tape of the performance and write it down later. It could be a welcome new addition to the act. You'd be surprised how many established comics will deliver a hilarious throw-away line on stage that just popped into their brain, and then after their set, race off stage to see if anyone remembered what they said.

Motivation for these inspired moments of ad-libbing often comes from give-and-take with the audience. The comedy audience accounts for half of the success or failure of a performance. You are the other half. A good crowd can make a average comedy show GREAT and a bad one could make it unbearable. Certainly your material will have some affect on the quality of the audience. Still even the top pros like Jay Leno can meet up with a bad group. The material is the same ... the audience reaction is less than it usually is. The comedian must work harder for laughs to compensate for the weakness in the crowd. There is a danger here of placing the blame for a failed set on the audience. This is a bad practice to get into. Any comic worth his or her weight should be able to work any crowd for at least satisfactory results and, in the event of the off-night, be able to walk away from the experience without expressing any animosity towards the questionable group.

The Heckler

The prime "cheerleader" and "principle spokesman" of this questionable group is of course "The Heckler." Let's face it gang, they're out there. They've been a fact of life for performers since time began and they show little sign of letting up. As long as there have been stages for performers to work on, there have been audience seats for hecklers to yell from. Shakespeare even probably had to deal with hecklers. Of course, he didn't have the modern, state of the art heckler lines we have today to deal with the problem. However, "Is that your face or did your neck throw up" probably wouldn't have worked well in "Hamlet" anyway.

Since each comedian has their own comic stage persona, each has his or her own special way of dealing with these cheeseball duffusses known as hecklers. As you perform on your open mikes, you'll begin to pick out these herring-brained sheep lovers. Expect them. They are an unfortunate part of the biz. Discover your own unique way of dealing with these motor-mouthed dirtclods. There are standard heckler lines in the comedy community that you can use to rid yourself of these one-celled, enema-loving nuisances. "I don't go to McDonalds and bother you while you're working," "I was going to do my impression of an asshole, but you beat me to it," "Gee, it's too bad we don't have microphones for EVERYBODY" ... there are many more. You may even write your own heckler material. Have a few lines tucked away in your brains at all times. Picture them next to an axe in a glass case with a sign saying "In case of emergency...". More than likely, you'll get a big laugh with a heckler line and the audience will cheer you on. Don't confuse this with having a good set. Heckler lines are seldom a regular part of a comic's set and you should never depend on them to make or break your act. If anything, hecklers should make you angry! They've interrupted you, your set and the audience. All of your timing has been thrown out the window. Now you have to go out of your way and deal with this moron. You may try to establish some rapport with them to get them to shut up. But often it takes a low-shot heckler line to do it. Sometimes several heckler lines. Sometimes MANY heckler lines. By this point, you could be running your whole set around one jerk ... this creep in the audience. Your set is ruined. The audience may be laughing at these stock heckler lines, but they'll never get to hear your original material which is vastly more worthy of their attention. Many times in these cases, the manager will throw the bum out. But not always. Just don't count on it. The crowning point comes when this lowlife, fish smelling, empty brained epitomy of nothingness comes backstage and suggests to you that he was a big help to your set. Capitol punishment may be used in these certain cases.

Reciting an endless stream of heckler lines is not the only way to handle these jerks. Sometimes, the best method is to simply ignore them. Throwing the entire attention of the show onto one disident audience member can backfire on you. Instead of embarrassing them, you might be stroking their ego by acknowledging them, even if it's with the best put down heckler line in the biz. This might just inflame additional responses from the heckler, or worse, spread to other would-be hecklers in the audience. By ignoring him and continuing on with your performance, the heckler might just quietly saunter off to obscurity.

Comic Interview: **Karen Anderson**

How long have you been in comedy?
>Close to 3 years

What comics influenced you?
>Steve Martin, Paula Poundstone (a lot!)

Any advice for a new comic?
>If a joke doesn't go over, act like that's how it's supposed to
>be and move on! Have confidence!

What makes you a funny person?
>Attention to detail. When I was 15, I had head gear, braces,
>glasses, weighed 90 pounds at 5'8" and wore a back brace! I
>had to be funny!

How has comedy benefited you?
>I can be a geek in public. It's a great outlet. I've met some
>of my best friends. It really takes care of all my creative
>wants. And of course, all that money.

What is the future of comedy?
>Clubs are going to be around forever. Seeing a live
>performance will never die. Women are going to be doing
>stand-up more and more.

Any additional comments?
>There isn't another job that gives you immediate response in
>laughter for something you personally wrote.

No matter how bad a crowd you get, there is one golden rule in comedy that has applied from vaudeville until today..."The Show Must Go On!" This open mike period in your career will often put you at your most vulnerable. After every failed set, you might have the urge to throw your three notebooks of material and yourself out of the nearest highrise. Stop yourself from this at all costs. The fines for littering alone would financially strap you for decades. Every comedian from Chaplin to Lenny to today's comic stars has had a period of dues paying. If you find yourself sobbing at night over a ten minute comedy bit that crashed and burned, do one of two things. Either get out of the business and get some psychological help or realize that this comedy apprenticeship program can last two to three years. Nobody expects you to headline after three weeks of tough one nighter open mikes, and everyone has gone through what you're going through. Don't give yourself high expectations that can't possibly be filled. With each open mike, refine your set and build new material. Use these crash and burn sets as a learning experience and don't loose hope. The only comedians who ever made it in this business were the ones who said "Don't Give Up" and had the confidence, patience and sheer guts to wait out this long, learning period.

If you've mastered and grown tired of playing your local comedy club's open mike, it may be time to spread your comedy wings and venture out to other areas. As we mentioned earlier in this chapter, comedy clubs are everywhere and open mikes are plentiful in many cities. Contact all the clubs in your outlying areas about performing at their open mikes. Mention to them that you have the experience at your local club. With persistance, you may be able to get a spot. Take off an hour early from work and drive the three hour drive to the club. Do your set. Drive the same three hour drive home and go back to work on three hour's sleep. This practice will run you ragged, but it's one that is common to many comics in the beginning of their careers. The idea of course is to play as many open mikes as possible. You may find a great demographic and intellectual difference in the crowd at each different club you play. You'll also have a better gauge for your material as you open up to different audiences. Make contacts with each club's operators and nurture with them the same professional relationship you've established with your local club. Not only will this give you the reputation of a hungry, upcoming comic but also as a mature business person.

Do your best set possible at this new club. Attempt to make a good impression on the club operator. This will be important for getting additional open mike slots in the future. Realize that these operators know that you are new to comedy. They're not looking at you as a 50 minute, triple A headliner. In our experience when we look at young, relatively inexperienced comics for the first time, we look for the sincerity of the performer. A comic who does ten very long, silent minutes on stage and then walks off with an attitude will not get far with us. Even though they laid a bomb that the Defense Department would be jealous of, they still are cocky and self-enamored. They are happy to let us know that "They killed the crowd" or "They were a stupid audience" or, the best one yet, "I'm not used to playing just ten minute sets." We are much more interested in comics who work on improving their material after a rough set. They're the ones asking questions to fellow comics or club managers and owners on how to spark up their act. They're the ones who are listening to their tape recorded sets and making notes. They're the ones who are watching the other acts on the show and looking for professional touches. They're the ones who are serious about becoming a quality comedian. These people are paying their dues for learning purposes, not for getting free drinks at the bar. If a club operator knows you are working hard at improving yourself, they will more than likely be receptive to keeping you on the open mike rotation as long as it takes for you to get to a professional level in comedy.

Hustle and play all of the open mikes at clubs within a decent range of your local base. The more open mikes you do at different clubs, the more contacts you'll make. Contacts are another "payoff" for this period in your career. Besides the knowledge and experience you're gaining about stand-up, you're meeting people who will have

a considerable bearing on your future success in comedy. Some of these clubs might be several of your first professional gigs. When a club operator believes you have progressed to a certain level, they may ask if you'd like to MC at an open mike. This is a wonderful opportunity for stage time and in some cases even pays a modest sum. From your experience as an open mike comic, you've learned how important the MC is to a comedy show. Now the responsibility is resting on your shoulders. It's reassuring to know that the club manager or owner has put enough faith in you and your material to do this very important job. They recognize that you have a decent ten to fifteen minutes of material and that you appear competent and professional. Your attitude has also made a good impression on them. They know you are serious about your work and that you are worthy of their trust. As an MC, you're expected to make sure that the evening's performance moves along at a steady clip. Different clubs will operate in different ways especially in regards to running open mike nights. You may be asked to do little more than introduce the acts. On the other hand, you may be expected to time the acts and give the signal light to them in addition to performing yourself. Talk to the club manager early on about how you can help out the show and what your evening's responsibilities are.

You'll also want to ask the scheduled comics about information for their introductions. Write the performers names and intro comments in order of appearance on a small card that can be discreetly brought on stage. Make sure each comic has prior knowledge of who they're following. You don't want to be running around trying to find someone who's about to go on stage.

As you begin to MC an open mike, start as usual by acknowledging the crowd with "good evenings" and "how are you doing to night." Let the audience know that they're going to have a great time. Tell them that there are three billion comics waiting to perform tonight. It's a very big show. Depending upon the management's instructions, you may have to do some commercials early on. Maybe you'll introduce the food and drink menu to the crowd or tell them about a special of the evening. Very often, you'll be asked to make a strong pitch for tips for the wait staff. Maybe it does begin to sound like a capitalistic, commercial sell-out, but try to remember that it's necessary to the successful running of a comedy club, and as an MC, you're expected to drum up business. Do whatever you can to help the boss (the manager or club owner) within reason. They'll be paying you tonight. Besides there will be plenty of time during the evening for you to perform your comedy.

Comic Interview: **Tim Wiggins**

How long have you been in comedy?
    5 years
Any advice for a new comic?
    No matter what, don't give up and kill yourself. It can really ruin a show.
What makes you a funny person?
    I have eyes, emotions and a brain; they seldom harmonize.
How has comedy benefited you?
    It's cheaper than morphine.
What is the future of comedy?
    There is no comedy in heaven, nobody needs it. On this earth, I've no idea what the future is.
Any additional comments?
    Life is too mysterious, bizarre and intense to joke about. Thank God for 7-11's, cats and dogs, relationships, blah, blah, blah ...

During your first few minutes on stage, before, in-between or after your commercials for the club, do some of your best material. Establish yourself as a performer, not just a pitch-person for the room. Get the crowd going. Warm them up. Get them used to laughing! Even though you might be doing terrific, remember that there are three billion comics back stage waiting to come out. After your scheduled time, prepare to introduce the first act.

As we mentioned earlier, the MC's introduction to an act is very important. The audience responds warmer to a comic who has been given an energetic, uplifting introduction. Don't just say "here's so and so". Tell them where the comic is from. Give the audience any recent credits the comic might have. Consider adding a personal note such as "I think this guy is very funny" or "You guys are gonna love this next act." Then with an uptempo manner, invite the audience to "Please welcome *So and So!*" Walk off stage shaking hands with the act. Throughout this entire process, you are conveying to the audience verbally and non-verbally that they are going to enjoy this next performer. You're also letting the audience know that you respect the performer as a professional and that they should too.

With practice as an MC, you'll begin to loosen up. Act like this is your show. Pretend that you're Ed Sullivan and you're bringing out Topo Gigio. In between sets, you may want to do a little material. This comes in handy especially after a comic who might have bombed. Use some routines which will bring the audience back. Remember that you are responsible for consistent quality throughout the show and more than likely, you'll be expected to make up for the weaker acts.

At the end of each set, reappear on stage shaking hands with the performer and asking the audience to continue applauding for *So and So*. This enables you to get the act's name out one last time so that those in the audience who wish to do so can remember it.

Continue interspersing your material among your introductions to the acts. Keep the show lively and at a good pace. When it comes time to end the show, mention several important things. Number one, thank the audience for coming to the show and being a great crowd. Number two, remind the audience again to tip beverage and food servers. Number three, ask audience members to tell their friends about the great time they had at the club. And finally, number four, ask the audience to give a big round of applause for all of the acts that appeared on the show. (In the future, when you begin to MC standard three act shows, it is recommended to recall all of the performers names. This need not be done when MC'ing open mikes because of the amount of acts.) As the audience is applauding, tell the audience "good night" and ask them to "come back again." This way, you walk off stage on applause and also close the show on an upbeat note.

The more open mikes you do, the more chances you'll have for exposure. You will get to a certain level where you'll begin to meet all of the local comics in your area. You'll be familiar with all of the clubs and club owners. Your name will begin to circulate throughout the comedy community. People may begin to notice you. As you become a regular fixture on the open mike circuit, bookers may begin to consider you for paying gigs, other than MC'ing. This exciting moment can only happen after a reasonable amount of open mike stage experience. Consider this scenario... open mike gigs are like buying lottery tickets. The more you get, the better odds you have at achieving your next goal: PAYING GIGS!

Chapter Six:
Making Contacts

"It's not what you know, it's who you know."

We hear that expression in every business. In comedy, it also applies. Making contacts in this business is essential to enjoying a successful career. You have the power to open up opportunities for advancement every time you meet a new club owner or booking agent. These individuals rely on your previous experience to assist them in making their initial judgment of you as a possible performer for their stage. With your background of successful open mikes and MC'ing, you have grown into a valuable commodity. Through your patience and perseverance, you have elevated yourself and your material to a professional level. You will now begin to reap some minor monetary rewards as you begin to embark on your first paying gigs, some of which might be at the very clubs where you open miked. Once you've mastered these, it's time to let the rest of the comedy world "know you've arrived."

Think of yourself as an independent contractor. You are selling a service. You and your comedy set are an entity of value to prospective bookers and clubowners. They are always looking for new and talented acts. They are looking for you. You have to be prepared to promote yourself and let these people know that you're available. Your best salestool is "You."

Many potential bookers won't even give you the time of day until they've seen your act. A phone call to the club to set up a showcase or audition spot is a good way to introduce yourself to them. These spots are generally done in front of a comedy crowd before a scheduled show begins or perhaps even during an open mike night. Your success or failure in getting booked from this method falls on how well you do in this special set.

Establish a professional relationship with the booker, club owner or manager right at the start. Perform your best ten minute set. This is not a good time for trying out new material. DO NOT GO LONG! Do your scheduled and expected time.

There are only two outcomes to this activity ... you'll either be successful in achieving a booking or you won't. It's entirely possible that the booker may decline to offer you a spot at the present time. They may state that you're not ready yet. Don't argue the point with them. It may help to ask where you could be stronger in your set. They may offer some helpful advice. Before leaving, ask to set up another audition date at another time. Depending upon the booker, you might get a second chance.

On the more optimistic side, the booker might be suitably impressed by your performance and offer you a week long opening slot. Here's the moment you've been waiting for ... a chance for a real professional booking. The booker has enough faith in you that he or she believes you can do a decent twenty minute set. This will establish you as a PROFESSIONAL COMIC. Discuss the time frame of the available date with the booker. Make sure it will not conflict with your schedule. You don't want to have to cancel an initial booking. Doing so might give you a flakey reputation as far as this particular club is concerned. Before you leave the club, establish the date, location and showtimes of the gig. In addition, set the pay scale. Don't leave this up in the air. Write down the agreed amount of pay so that there will be no discrepancy when you get your check. Most clubs also provide some travel reimbursement funds as well as living accomodations for the week-long engagement. Establish this as well and make a note of it before you leave. Remember to call the booker approximately thirty days prior to the gig. At this time, you can confirm money, travel, accomodations and show schedules so that there will be no surprises on either side of the agreement. Contact the club one last time the week before your engagement to inform the club of your arrival time.

Comic Interview: Vince Champ

How long have you been in comedy?
     6 years
What comics influenced you?
     Eddie Strange, Bruce Baum, Al Clethan
Any advice for a new comic?
     Try a new bit everytime you step on stage.
What makes you a funny person?
     I think I have good stage presence and fairly original
     material as well as a good rapport with the audience.
How has comedy benefited you?
     Financially and self-fulfillment as well. I have reached
     several personal goals.
What is the future of comedy?
     Unlimited and I believe it is the tip of an iceberg. Plenty
     more movies and cable specials in the works.

As there are hundreds of potential bookings around the country, it is not particulary feasible to do guest audition sets for every club. It would take a virtual Harry Truman Whistle Stop train tour to get to every one. How fortunate we are to live in the video age! Thanks to VCR's, it is possible to "audition" for every national club and never leave town.

With a little bit of luck, you may have established a particulary friendly rapport with one special club owner from your open mike bookings. Hopefully, this club also has video taping facilities. Offer to pay for the opportunity to tape your set at the club. More than likely, they won't charge you a thing, as long as you provide a tape. Videotape a series of sets with different audiences on your open mikes. Choose the best set and have VHS copies made. You now have a video calling card that will put your best comedy foot forward.

Before mailing out your first video, you need two very important items. First, you should prepare an 8 X 10 inch black and white glossy photo of yourself. The 8 X 10's are a standard salestool in the comedy business. The ideal ones present a photo of you that best represents your stage persona. If you're the rough and rowdy type of comic, you might have an extremely off-the-wall pose. If you're more on the intellectual side, something more sedate might be in order. Make sure your photo is in character. The 8 X 10 should have a white border with your name, address and phone number at the bottom. Many photography studios offer this service. If you have trouble finding one, try checking with a local modeling agency. Best yet, try to ask a friend who might be into photography to help you out. Yes, the 8 X 10 is so important that you should shamefully use your friends for your own selfish personal gain!

Second, you should prepare a one page resume of your performance history, commonly referred to as a "bio." This brief statement should include your name, address, phone number and lists of previous gigs including any clubs you've played to give the booker a reference point to go by. You need not note every single club you ever played at. Point out the highlights. As your career continues, you'll add listings for bigger clubs, opening slots for established acts, radio TV and film appearances and so on. Keep your bio short and to the point. It's alright to write a little bit about yourself, but don't make a book out of it. Club booking agents are more interested in what you've been doing in your last six months than what you've been doing since birth.

IKE SCHWARTZ
Actor / Comedian

COMEDY CLUBS
HA HA'S, Mt. Holyoke, MA
HO HO'S, Punxatawny, PA
HEE HEE'S, Glen Arden, MD
HAR-DE-HAR-HAR'S, Beaumont, TX

CASINOS AND SHOWROOMS
ERNIE'S PLACE, Las Vegas

TELEVISION
THE TONIGHT SHOW
THE PAT SAJAK SHOW
THICKE OF THE NIGHT

FEATURE FILMS
HIGH SCHOOL HELL BOUND (Man on plane)
HARDBODIES (Man behind door)
ERNEST SAVES EL SALVADOR (Co-starring role)

After you've prepared your 8 X 10 and a bio, make calls to the clubs you want to play and request information on who to send the package to. Most clubs are eager to seek out new talent and are more than willing to take a look at your tape. Let the club know that the package is on its way so that they'll expect it and won't toss it in the trash when it comes in the mail.

In this initial stage, concentrate your submissions to limited geographical areas. If you're living in Seattle, send to clubs in the Pacific Northwest and the West Coast. Try to build a following in this concentrated area instead of spreading yourself out too thin across the country. There will be plenty of time for that later. This will also allow you to keep your day job as long as possible.

Send your package only to the clubs that request to see it. Along with your video, 8 X 10 and bio, insert a cover letter mentioning your previous conversation with the booker. Hopefully the booker will enjoy your tape and respond with a performance date. This may take a few weeks, so you must be patient. Club owners are sent dozens of tapes monthly. Your tape may take a while to be viewed as it joins the ever increasing pile of submissions. It will, however, eventually be judged. After several weeks, don't be afraid to call the club and check on the tape's status. You may even need to make a call once a week. Remember, the squeaky wheel gets the grease. However, don't be a pest. If you find yourself making daily calls and showing up at the club's door, you might be doing more harm than good.

When submitting video tapes, keep in mind that they are seldomed returned. You can best be assured that your tape will be returned if you send along a self-addressed stamped envelope with your package along with a written request asking for the return of your tape.

There are benefits and drawbacks to both the live guest set and video tape audition method. With a live guest set, you have an opportunity to meet the booker one to one and establish a personal relationship. It is possible to get a date on the night of your perform-ance! You also get a chance to evaluate the club and decide if this is the kind of place that YOU want to work at. Along with these great plusses come the minuses ... most notably, with a live guest set, you have one LIVE ten minute performance to determine the course of the impression you make on the booker. If you have an off-night, it might not put you in the best light. The live audition is certainly a test of your self-confidence. Additionally, the live audition calls for travel on your part. You must find your own way to the club, even though hours of travel may be involved, and naturally no pay or reimbursement is available.

The big plus to a tape set, of course, is the fact that you can audition anywhere, anytime at a minimum amount of investment. The costs of a video tape and postage can prove to be much less than travel costs. It is also possible to "audition" for more than one club at the same time as you are unlimited to the amount of places you can send tapes to. You also enjoy the benefit of selecting your best performance for view by the bookers. You're not subject to that "hit or miss ten minute LIVE set." Where are the minuses here? While the video method seems perfect, it can't replace a good one on one impression that can be made during a live audition with a booker. In addition, as we've seen earlier, video tapes in the quantity being sent to comedy clubs these days tend to stack up before they're viewed. When a booker finally goes through a stack of videos, one comic soon begins to merge into another and the long string of hopefuls seem to mold together into a monsterous "Star Search" show. When you audition live, you have the advantage of being in the booker's spotlight on the booker's home turf. You have the solitary, complete and total attention of the booker. Unlike the video method, there is no fast forward button at the booker's command to edit your audition. The video tape audition unfortunately offers you little control of your tape once it leaves your hands.

Making contacts in the comedy business is much the same as in any other business. There is an element of risk involved. Let the truth be known! Not all clubs and club owners / managers / bookers are created equal. There are ones who are honest, upright members of the comedy industry with high moral standards and professional reputations. Unfortunately, an element of sleaze also exists. This element consists of unscrupulous, piss brain, so-called "comedy-icons" who have big mouths with lots of promises and no paychecks. The comedy industry generally has an honesty agreement between club and performer that does not usually involve contracts and as such, relies mostly on vocal agreements and handshakes. As many comics are their own managers and agents, this rather loose way of doing business is seen as the most practical method and works fairly well with a minimum of complications. However, there is a small (thankfully very small) minority of club owners / bookers / managers who take advantage of this arrangement.

Your one great defense against these morons is your mouth and the mouths of your fellow comics. An owner / manager / booker who gains a reputation for backing-out on pre-agreed-to committments will soon be branded by the comedy community. Once word spreads that a certain club or booker is a rip-off, comics will stay away from them in multitudes. This clown soon won't be able to FIND a comic let alone hire one. If you have doubts about a club, ask a fellow comic. If you have a problem with a club, tell a fellow comic.

Happily, these sleaze balls are generally managing the sleazier clubs. Soon after a club gains a tainted reputation, the good comics stop appearing, the audiences stop coming, and another venue run by a reputable club owner springs up across town. The clubs run by crooks soon begin to die a slow, lingering death. The Comic's Revenge.

From our personal point of view, as club owners who've been in the business for years,   the advice we were given at the start still

Comic Interview: Stephanie Landers

What comics influenced you?
George Carlin, Lenny Bruce, David Letterman and Diane Nichols
Any advice for a new comic?
Invest in a small tape recorder and listen carefully to your performances. You'll learn a lot. When you see another comic, figure out what you like or dislike about their act and integrate or eschew those qualities (but never, ever steal! No one will ever take you seriously.) Finally wait for your laughs. Don't be so eager to spill out the bit and get on to the next one that you forgot the reason you're there.
How has comedy benefited you?
Comedy has benefited me by allowing me to vent my negative feelings in a socially acceptable way, e.g. people don't want to hear me scream about the stupidity of postal workers while standing in line at the P.O., but in a big, dark room with a live microphone and a spotlight on me, they feel they're getting their money's worth. Weird, but true. Plus, I get respect from surprising sources, like real cynical people.
What is the future of comedy?
Comedy has already become a cheap commodity, right up there with fast food. Look for this trend to continue. The current generation was raised on TV and now wants something that can't be prepackaged ... live performances. I don't believe that comedy will bottom out suddenly unless technology comes up with some new, really spiffy form of entertainment.

stands ... "you take care of the comics, they'll take care of you." This doesn't necessarily always equate to large sums of money, however. As many comics will tell you, we are not one of the highest paying clubs in the country. On the other hand, the checks are always good. We provide nice accomodations for our comics, offer multiple bookings and operate our rooms very professionally. Perhaps our biggest asset is the respect we offer to entertainers. Many comics tell stories of club owners who treat performers like dirt. We feel that this is very inappropriate since the performer's talents are the reason we're in this business in the first place. They are the product we are offering to the public and as such deserve to be treated in a professional manner. Many of the more prominent clubs in the country also subscribe to this theory.

Do some research yourself. Ask comics about the better clubs to play at. Even though your objective is to gain as much stage time as possible and to keep a full schedule, be a little picky. Never play a club with a bad rep. Always try to deal directly with the person who is booking you. Third party messages can create confusion. Always write down the agreement as soon as it's agreed to. And never, never accept a professional gig from someone you don't know for free (other than an open-mike or audition). If you don't have a prior relationship with a certain booker and they offer you a job without pay, they obviously don't respect you as a professional. If they're not willing to shell out a little bit of cash for your time, your time certainly means little to them. Get something ... ANYTHING. To be fair, some bookers might not have large funds available for bookings. Maybe they're really on a tight budget. Well, no one said you had to make a headliner's salary either. Ask for a small amount of cash and travel expenses along with comp food and drinks perhaps. Work with the booker if you really want the job. If they really want you, they'll work with you also.

Initially with first time bookings, monetary offerings might be relatively small. This doesn't necessarily mean you're being ripped off. A booker sometimes will offer less money to a newcomer simply because the performer hasn't yet proven himself in a week-long gig

situation. If this first week of performances works out well, re-bookings will certainly bring more money.

Remember, you are a *professional comedian* now. Approach your business dealings on this level. Make sure of all of the terms of the date and keep the information logged in your gig-notebook or calendar. Make sure your salary is appropriate. Make sure travel, if necessary, is included. Make sure the accomodations, if necessary, will be livable. For your part, plan to be on time. Make sure the club knows when you plan to arrive in town. And be funny! If something eventually conflicts with your scheduled date and you have to cancel your appearance, give the club at least a months notice.

Depending on your day job schedule, work as often as possible. The more contacts you make, the more work will result and the more experience you'll gain. It's not easy to handle a regular job during the day and a comedy career at night, but every comic has faced these same difficulties at some time. Be aggressive, professional and build confidence in yourself and your material. Hit the road with your twenty minutes and see what comes up.

Chapter Seven
"Such are the Sacrifices of the Road"

Aren't your Aunt Jim and Uncle Martha proud! You've become a professional comedian!!! Oh sure, it took a lot of hard work, learning and sacrifice to get to this stage, but it was all worth it. Now you just have to cruise down easy street until your big break comes in. Right?

Wrong!

At this point in your career, it's time to move onto comedy's "higher education" plateau. Since there is no "Comedy College" to mold comics into top professionals and to weed-out the would-be pros, something much more sinister and diabolical had to be developed. It's called "The Road."

Life on "The Road" can turn run of the mill comics into great comics. It forces others to look for other means of employment. The Road can be the greatest teacher ... and an extremely strict one. If you can survive The Road and learn from it, a successful comedy career is in your future.

Working comedy clubs week after week is what The Road is all about. Eventually, you want to get to the point where you find yourself performing in a different club in a different town every week.

Naturally, this can take its toll on your personal life. Many sacrifices must be made, but the experience you'll gain will more than make up for them.

Though each comedy club is different, you'll find certain industry standards existing throughout. Most clubs today subscribe to the three act format consisting of a headliner, middle act, opening act, as well as a regular club MC. The standard three act comedy club show is roughly a two hour performance. The opening act is generally given twenty minutes. A middle act has a slightly longer scheduled time of a half hour. The Headliner, the "star of the show", is scheduled for forty five to fifty minutes or more! The MC rounds out the evening, filling in time at the beginning of the show and between each act.

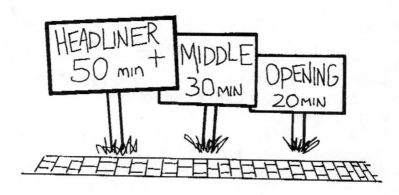

At many clubs, the opening act will also perform all of the MC duties. Like any good MC should, their objective is to warm up the audience and to start the excitement level building in the room. They'll open up the show by welcoming the crowd to the club and letting them know who is on the show for the evening. The opening act / MC should encourage applause after they announce each performer's name, even though it's most likely that the audience has never heard of them. All of the standard MC'ing rules apply. Since you've had ample experience from your days at open mikes, you should perform this function quite nicely. Unfortunately, being a combination opening act / MC has its down side.

Part of the difficulty in being an opening act / MC is finding a way to segue from your MC chores to your original material. You don't have the benefit of someone announcing your name on stage, which would allow you to come out to an applauding audience and begin your set immediately. Instead, you might find yourself talking about drink specials and then trying to smoothly move into material about your Ford Escort. The audience at times will have trouble discovering when the commercials stop and when your set begins. You have to convince the audience that you are a full fledge comic, and not some flunky from the staff who's trying to tell jokes in between making club announcements. Not an easy task, but one that must be mastered.

There is a bright side of course. The benefit of being an opening act / MC is the advantage of increased stage time. In addition to your regular twenty minute set, you're also expected to appear on stage before and after the other acts ... introducing them and later-bringing them off to thunderous applause. Before you introduce each comic, you can perform a small amount of material. Keep in mind though that it is not appropriate to add material after the headliner's set. Once a headliner (the "star of the show") is through, the show is over. Don't attempt to upstage the headliner by performing material after their act. All that is necessary is to re-appear on stage and ask for the customary server tips, invite the audience to tell their friends about the show and bring the show to an end by encouraging applause for all of the acts while mentioning their individual names. Say goodnight to the crowd as the applause continues.

Sometimes, comedy clubs hire house MC's that appear regularly every night. At these gigs, the opening act is relieved of their MC chores. They then have the advantage of performing their act free and clear of any other responsibilities. In regards to their relationship with the audience, this is much more preferable to the performer. When you hit the stage, you are seen as a featured comedian in the eye of the audience as opposed to giving the impression that you're an MC who happens to do a little comedy on the side. Your credibility is enhanced and you don't have to worry about pushing drinks and food either.

Your efforts in submitting your video tape, photo and bio promotion package or performing guest set auditions will hopefully allow you to acquire these week-long comedy gigs. As a new comic on the circuit with a small amount of experience, chances are you'll start at a club as an opening act. It is extremely rare that you'd start at any other position. Ideally these initial club dates should be close enough to home to allow you to live a double life. At the beginning, you may find yourself driving back and forth to the club every night and working every day at your regular job. You might end up using well-deserved vacation time performing in obscure out-of-town clubs. Such are the sacrifices of The Road.

Whether you're an opener, a middle act or a headliner, working these week long comedy gigs isn't much different from any other comedy experience you've had up to this point. The regular rules of being on time, knowing your scheduled time, not getting drunk, not bothering the staff, not being cocky to managers or other comics and keeping a professional attitude at all times are still recommended. The main difference in working a week long gig will be your life off-stage.

When you're on The Road, you have the great fortune or misfortune of having to live with other comics. Sharing a dwelling with comics can be a great time ... or a disaster. Perhaps your first few week long gigs will be located in your local or regional area which will allow you to drive to and from the club nightly. Naturally in this case, you'll have the benefit of sleeping in your own bed in your own home. After a time on The Road, you'll appreciate how wonderful this can be. If your gig will not allow you this benefit, your alternative is life at the "Comedy Condo." Roughly, this can be like living in a college dorm all over again.

Your roommates are the other comics on the weekly bill. Assuming that you're the opening act for the week, you'll be living with the middle act and the headliner. All clubs have different accomodations planned for their entertainers, but one fact is consistant. You are the opening act ... you're at the bottom of the proverbial totem pole ... you're not going to get the cushiest arrangements. You'll find that the headliner will do the best of the bunch, probably getting his or her own room with a king size bed. The middle act will do OK having perhaps their own room with a smaller bed. You as the opening act will probably sleep on the sofa or room with the middle act. Regardless of the club's standard sleeping accomodations, the headliner will always have the first choice of preferable sleeping arrangements. After all, they are "the star of the show." They'll probably remind you of that if you beg to question the justice of it all. You're the opening act. You take what's left.

Remember, you have never met, spoken to, or in most cases ever heard of these people before. Now you're going to attempt to LIVE with them for an entire week. Such are the sacrifices of The Road.

In most cases, the comedy condo set-up works fine. You'll be surprised to learn that many comics regardless of professional stature are just like you. They want as stable a living condition on The Road as possible. They want to make it bearable too. They may not want to stay up till all hours of the night partying. They may not care to have McDonalds every evening for dinner. They might enjoy peace and quiet. But beware! The "Road Animals" are out there! These comics are terrific people, but they enjoy an extremely lively flair in their off-hours. Activities could include inviting the entire comedy club audience over to the condo after the show. They might be the type to invite the local pimps and hookers in the area over for an intriguing discussion on tribal mating rituals. At the very least, these comics might find it necessary to play their boom boxes at ear-splitting volume at four in the morning. These comics are graduates from the "Keith Moon School of Social Etiquette" and are of course a totally charming, fun-loving group who might have been your best friends in high school, but you never imagined having to live with them! Now you're getting paid to.

Always try to make life as pleasant as possible in the condo. If a fellow comic wants to keep to his or herself, don't be a pest. Give each other the space you would want. You're not living under the best of conditions so don't make it worse by being a pain in the butt. One problem that comedians often experience when living with their colleagues is having to put up with a roommate comic who is "on" all the time. These performers don't leave their comic stage persona on the

83

stage at the comedy club. They act wacky, nutty, goofy, crazy, dopey, and zany on stage AND OFF! They consider it a necessity to continue performing around the clock, even to their fellow comics in the condo. This is especially true of new comics who feel they have to prove to the veterans that they too are funny. This can get old real fast. Try to act as normal as possible outside of the comedy club and make life bearable for your roommates.

Likewise, life at the condo can be great. You could end up with a fantastic bunch of comics. You might find yourself having a great time passing the off hours with your new pals. There are movies to see, restaurants to eat at and golf courses to try. You could have group discussions on the day's "Gilligan's Island" repeat. You can watch MTV all day long and count the number of Madonna videos. You can pretend you're on "Family Affair" and take turns being "Buffy". With your luck, you'll end up as "Mr French." Such are the sacrifices of The Road.

Living with and around comics has one advantage especially for new comedians. There is ample opportunity to gain additional knowledge about the comedy industry. Comics often divulge their past experiences to other comics on The Road. You might gain some constructive criticism on your act. You might even find yourself writing material with a fellow comic. You are living in a comedy environment and some of this will rub off on you. After a while, you'll begin to mature as a comedian.

As you perform at the club during the week, you'll notice certain patterns in the audiences. These are common in all comedy clubs across the country. For example, the weeknight shows are generally slower. You may be playing to half a house or less and the atmosphere is generally more relaxed. These are good nights to work on new material. However, don't do an entire set of new stuff ... never open up a set with something that's never seen the light of day ... simply float the new bits in with your proven material somewhere in the middle of the act. On these nights, if a new joke bombs, who cares?! As long as you have good material ready to back you up, these

84

weeknight shows can offer you the opportunity to be more adventurous on stage.

However, it's a different ball game on Friday and Saturday nights. These are the big nights for the club ... and for you. These are also known as "bill paying nights" to club owners. There are full houses in the room. VIPs are perhaps in the audience. This is not the time for fooling around. Don't "wing it" or try massive amounts of new material here. You want to make your best impression possible to this packed house. The club's reputation and YOUR reputation hang in the balance. On these big nights, you have the opportunity to widen your fan base. By performing your best sets to a full house, you'll begin to improve your "drawing power." Next time you appear at the club, people may come to see YOU!

Most clubs schedule two shows on Friday and Saturday nights, so it's VERY critical to keep tight on your time. This is especially true on the Friday Late Show. Imagine you've been working hard all day and after work, you decide to go out with your friends to the local pub. You have six stiff ones and you think you're feeling great. In a drunken frenzy and to top off the evening, you and your pals decide to head over to the comedy club for a late Friday show! You can bet that the majority of the audience members in any given late Friday show are in this state. They're tired from working and stupid from drinking. This is the audience that you and your fellow comics will be facing. This crowd is a ticking time bomb ... the longer the show runs, the more tired and stupid they'll get. Obviously, this will not be the best show of the week. If you, as an opening act, go long on this show, you'll be forcing the other comics (i.e. your "roomates") to play to an increasingly tougher crowd. By the time the headliner goes on, the show will be running late and the crowd could be acting like an unruly mob. (A dream come true for any comic.)

Just as the Friday Late Show is usually horrible, the early show on Saturday is usually the best of the week. Odds are that the show has been sold out for days. These audience members have planned early on for the show and to them, this is a big event! They haven't even begun their evening's drinking yet. You've got two great ingredients for a terrific audience here ... people who are very enthusiastic about seeing a comedy show and people without booze! More than likely, this will be the easiest audience to perform to. They'll be very receptive to you and your material. You'll be tempted to stay on stage because you're doing so well. Of course, as a professional, you'll know not to go long. As Saturday is a two show night, the show must end at a pre-determined time to allow seating for the next audience. Going long will cut into the time available for the other comics (your roommates)!

The remainder of the weekend shows will run somewhere in quality between these two extremes. Remember when you're working on a three act show, you're part of a team. Show courtesy to the other comics by sticking to your scheduled time and maybe they won't make you sleep outside tonight.

As a general rule, most clubs pay immediately after the last show. Make sure that you've been paid the proper amount and received acceptable travel reimbursements. Don't ever let a club say that they are going to "mail you a check" unless you're sure of their reputation. Many clubs will offer to pay out a little in cash in addition to a check with the balance. With a busy comic's schedule, it might take several days before you can make it to the bank and banking institutions have a nasty habit of holding checks for ten days. Cashing an entire check at the club will generally not meet with much enthusiasm from the boss, but don't hesitate to ask for fifty or a hundred dollars to get you through until banking day. Any reputable club should have no problem with this request.

Some clubs also are available for re-bookings after the last show. This is a good time to get out your gig book and schedule additional dates. At this point, it's acceptable to ask for a small increase in salary. You've proven yourself. Now you should start making a little more cash. Negotiate with the booker in good faith and

work out a suitable deal with some give and take on both sides. Write down the information in your scheduling book and end the transaction. If for some reason it's not possible to do any booking on your last

Comic Interview: Willie Tyler *(of Willie Tyler and Lester)*

How long have you been in comedy?
     Over thirty years
What comics influenced you?
     Ventriloquist Paul Winchell, Johnny Carson, Redd Foxx
Any advice for a new comic?
     You've got to want to do it, even when you don't feel like doing it.
What makes you a funny person?
     I'm a ventriloquist. Lester makes me funny.
How has comedy benefited you?
     Comedy keeps me happy and feeling young.
What is the future of comedy?
     Lots of laughs (hopefully).

night, make sure to call for a date within the next seven days so that you and your act will be fresh in the booker's mind.

Before leaving the condo, leave the keys with the arranged person. The condo is an important part of a comedy club operation and the care you've taken of it reflects on your employment future with the club. You were a guest of the club and you stayed at the club's property, no matter how modest. Comics that trash condos, steal towels and show little respect for the dwelling will NEVER work that club again.

If you are like most comics, you'll leave this gig for the next immediately. Mondays are set aside as travel days and you'll find yourself preparing to move to the next town on your itinerary. If possible, many comics try to swing by home even if it's out of their way. This allows them to check messages and mail, pay bills, book club dates and take care of other domestic chores. If you do this, keep in mind that you are responsible for getting to your next gig in plenty of time to be fresh and ready for another week of comedy.

Continue sending out your promotional packages and performing the occasional live audition guest set. From your initial regional base, begin to spread your submissions out further and further across the country. It is still recommended to stay somewhat regional ... that is, west coast, east coast, mid west, etc. This will help you obtain a regional following that is important in building momentum at the start of a career. Book yourself intelligently. Try to arrange bookings geographically if possible. For example, if you know that you're playing a week in Chicago, try contacting clubs in surrounding cities for additional work for the following weeks. If you're going to the trouble to travel for one gig, why not get two out of it. Or three. Pretty soon, you've arranged your very own "Comedy Tour"!

This is all fine and well for comics with no responsibilities who are care free and basically homeless. But what about the new comics who still are tied to their bills and day jobs. You might find yourself in a situation where some tough choices have to be made.

Eventually, assuming you are talented and have been working hard at your craft for a number of years, you will obtain such a substantial amount of week long comedy club offers that the prospect of quitting the day job and going into comedy full time will begin to surface. The decision to quit the day job can only be made after you're sure you can acquire enough steady work as a comic to a least take care of your bills and responsibilities. Naturally the pay at first will be minimal and you'll probably be on a tight budget. Think of this before you commit yourself. Remember that many comics work for years before giving up the income of a steady job. Pick the right time to make the change. Keep in mind that simply because you've landed one or two club gigs out of town doesn't mean you should throw your security away.

However, if you've discovered that it is possible to gain enough steady work to make ends meet, by all means GO FOR IT! It's an established fact that if you truly want to get to the top of the comedy ladder, you'll have to say goodbye to the Nine To Five routine sooner or later. Let's face it. No one was ever discovered while flipping burgers at McDonalds. Without the rope burns of a day job and a cozy home tying you down, you can virtually perform everywhere. You can say goodbye to wives/husbands/girlfriends/boyfriends for weeks at a time. You can begin to forget what a home cooked meal was all about. Of course the food was always rotton and that lousy, scum-sucking wife/husband/girlfriend/boyfriend was getting ready to drop you anyway. Sometimes, The Road really isn't so bad.

Working The Road is the comic's best educational experience. A good comic will never admit that they've learned everything there is to know about comedy, and The Road offers a new lesson every week. Working new clubs with different comics and new environments can only expand your knowledge of the comedy business. Playing consistently week after week will greatly improve your style, material, timing, professionalism and everything that will eventually mold you into a top performer.

Now that you're officially on "The Road," the way to success is Work Work WORK! (And More Work!) This is not a good time to get lazy. You are now YOUR OWN BOSS! You have started your own business! Your act is your product. You are your own sales staff, distributor, booking agent, promotion person and quality control expert. You are the lone responsible party for your career's success or failure. It's important to motivate yourself. Do something for your career everyday ... write a joke, punch up a bit, get a booking, whatever! Take charge of your career's destiny and push yourself to the comedy limits. It's true. The loneliness and pace of The Road can wear on you, but it's truly The Road to success.

Chapter Eight
The Comedy Ladder

   Success in comedy is achieved in stages. You advance in these stages by your ability to improve as a performer. As in any other job, while some people advance quickly, others seem to stay at a single level throughout their career. In comedy, there are comics who are opening acts, who have been opening acts for years and who will always be opening acts. There are those who have become headliners and have never left the comedy club circuit. There are those who continue to play just their regular clubs and don't wish to expand their schedules. If this is their plan, fine. But if not, problems may result. Being stuck at one level of the comedy ladder for any extended length of time can be frustrating and lead to severe depression. The ones who survive have the patience to endure these career lulls. There are ways to improve your career status, achieve your goals and continue climbing the comedy ladder. These may involve further sacrifices, but since by now you've thrown away any semblance of a normal life and have submitted yourself to the comedy gods, you are in a position to make them with a minimum amount of strain.

   Your best course of action at this stage in your career is to move up <u>steadily</u> on the comedy ladder. Too big of a step could have disasterous results. Let's look at your career up to this point. You're way past your open mike days. That's good. You've been performing in the opening act slot on a regular basis for the past year and a half or so. You're booked consistently and you're on the road three out of four weeks every month. You're beginning to be considered for middle slots and have indeed performed in that capacity at a few clubs. Your new material is advancing nicely and you're rarely doing any of your older pieces. Your new bits are much funnier. Financially, you're beginning to reap top dollar for opening acts. Yes it is time for a change. But what?

Your first change and primary goal at this point is to get off the opening act rung on the ladder. If you can move to the middle slot at most of your gigs, you'll increase, perhaps even double your income. To get to this stage, we suggest spicing up your promotion package. We're talking about new 8 X 10's, updating your bio and shooting a new video tape. You've grown as a comic over the last couple of years and your promotion package should reflect that fact. A new 8 X 10 will offer bookers a fresh look at you. Maybe you've sharpened your image. You might not look so "green" anymore. You're no longer the new kid who's trying to do comedy. You look more confident now, representing your new found self-assurance. Since your mom didn't take this photo and you've had it done by a professional studio, your appearance is much more impressive ... a night and day difference from your old photo. This is you as you are NOW ... the new and improved version.

Now let's take a look at your bio. Since your last version, you've added many new clubs to your list. These are all of the clubs you've been playing over the last two years with whom you've had successful relations. You've performed opening slots well at all of them and been re-booked by most. Perhaps you've even done some one-nighters here and there. The highlights of these credits should all be featured on your new bio, replacing the older, less-than-thrilling gigs on your original. Changing your St. Charles Bazarre and Mrs. Biggley's Tupperware Party performing credits to better quality listings will give your bio a more impressive look.

Most importantly, you should record a new video tape. Since

your first one was made, you've written all of this great new material and have virtually abandoned your original act. Your new tape will reflect this. You'll show bookers a more confident performer who's using brighter, funnier material with a greater performing flair. Your improved confidence is visable all over this new video. You're beginning to show bookers that you are becoming a middle act.

Comic Interview: **Bruce Baum**

How long have you been in comedy?
> Since 1973

What comics influenced you?
> Chaplin, Keaton, Woody Allen, Warner Brothers cartoon directors Chuck Jones, Bob Clampett and Robert McKimson

Any advice for a new comic?
> Do it as much and wherever you can.

What makes you a funny person?
> My DNA.

How has comedy benefited you?
> I'm excused from social graces.

After you've done several opening slots at any given club, ask the booker during negotiations for future dates about moving you up to a middle act. If the booker feels that you can do it, they'll more than likely give you a chance. They've seen your improvement first hand and your professionalism and commitment to the business has given them a trusting relationship with you. They will put their faith in you by moving you up to the middle slot. For those clubs that haven't hired you yet, send out your new, updated promotion package. When you book yourself, tell them that you're a middle act now and you're performing in that slot on a regular basis. They may be skeptical even after seeing your video. Don't argue with them over it. Make a deal. Tell them you'll accept an opening slot at an opening act's salary to give them a chance to see you. If they like what they see, your next booking can be a middle slot. This "one step backwards, two steps forwards" method is a fair way to begin working new clubs.

If you have fears of bookers keeping you in one position regardless of how great you're becoming, fear not! A good booking agent will put you in the proper place on the bill. For example, it wouldn't do the show any good to keep you at an opening act position if you're killing the crowd and doing extremely well. The middle act would have trouble following you! The show's momentum would screech to a grinding halt, slowing everything down and making it ultimately tougher on the headliner.

When your material and your act are ready, you will be moved up! Don't worry about that. There are those rare cases where the booker is an idiot and doesn't recognize a comic's true abilities. If you find yourself facing this, get outta there! There are plenty of other clubs to work. You might try asking the booker what the problem is and see if there's anything that can be done to improve the situation. Maybe they'll have some good advice ... maybe not. But if they still insist on keeping you as an opening act even though you're middling everywhere else, stop working that club for awhile. Eight months to a year later, contact the club again and see if they'd reconsider.

The logical step after quitting your day job and performing comedy full time would be to pull up stakes all together and move to an area which would benefit your career potential to a greater extent. There are several "comedy capitals" in the country at the present time. The most obvious of course are the New York and Los Angeles / Hollywood areas. Other cities such as Boston, San Francisco and Seattle have developed large comedy communities. Just as care was taken in finding the proper time for quitting your day job, equal care must be taken before moving on to one of these areas. Many new comics feel a need to move to New York or L.A. as soon as possible and, indeed, some enjoy modest success. However, we urge you to "try the act on the road first" before moving into these large areas. While relocating to a large entertainment center such as L.A. or New York is a promising proposition and eventual necessity, making the move to these areas too early can cause more harm than good for many comics.

The prospects at first look good in these cities. There are hundreds of places to perform. There are big-time agents mulling through the clubs at all times looking for new talent. The opportunities for greater stardom certainly are there. But before you pack your suitcase, realize this. For every single comedy club out of the hundreds that are open in these areas, there are potentially thousands of performers vying for spots on the bill. The competition is ferocious and the built-in seniority enjoyed by veteran comics who are already performing in these comedy capitals makes it extremely tough for a beginning comic to get a break. It is also a common practice in these large areas to set the pay scale at a minimum level ... even for top acts! Comics who might command decent salaries around the country's comedy clubs are working for less in L.A. and New York. We'll touch on this later. If you're a newcomer with an opening act and you've already bought your ticket to L.A., maybe you can go out to see Disneyland. Don't bother moving there. Yet.

However, a move of some sort is in order. Your material is strong enough and you're willing to take a chance in a different city! With your increased status to the middle slot position, you may be able to afford to move to a bigger comedy center. Let's say for example that you presently live in Denver. Even though you've been doing fine from this location, it wouldn't hurt you to move to an area where your comedy could achieve a more influencial visability. Our advice is to consider a Middle Market such as the Boston or San Francisco areas. These are sort of stepping stones to New York and L.A. and they offer large comedy communities and important contacts. Naturally, these are also expensive areas to live in. You may have to live cheap for awhile or move to the outlying areas.

There is a certain amount of loss in this move. Back in your home town, you were considered something of a novelty. The local comedian! You were a big fish in a small pond. When you move to a city with a comedy industry the size that San Francisco has, you've suddenly become a small fish in a BIG pond. This may be a culture shock at first, but in the long run as always, the sacrifice will be worth it. Your objective must be to penetrate this new city's inner circle of comedy.

Now that your performing mostly as a middle act, you're beginning to bring home enough cash from The Road to pay the bills. On your weeks off, you're starting to make contacts at some of the larger clubs in your new area. Consider your present position in a city the size of San Francisco much the same as if you were starting over doing open mikes. Do plenty of showcases. Offer to take the less-paying opening or MC'ing slots. Attempt to develop a following in the area. As you prove yourself to the local club owners, you'll begin to climb in stature up San Francisco's own comedy ladder.

After a period of hard work and steady gigs throughout the comedy club circuit both on the road and in San Francisco, you'll notice you're advancing in your career. Look back. You were an opening act back home. Then a middle act. Then an opening act on The Road. Then a middle act. Finally you were an opening act in San Francisco and now you're beginning to prove yourself to be a middle act there too. If you can middle in San Francisco, you might be able to headline back home!

Consider entering comedy competitions. These have recently become quite popular throughout the industry. At this stage, it would be advisable to enter as many competitions as possible. From the comic's fiscal standpoint, it's kind of a rip-off. You basically work for free ... sometimes several times. But opportunities for advancement in your career will make up for it. Competitions usually bring out big crowds and the press is always invited. You'll meet booking agents and influential people. If you're fortunate to become a finalist, you might even receive some national industry publicity. Being able to state that you were a finalist in any competition no matter how small makes a nice addition to your bio.

As you become more comfortable in the middle slot position in an area like San Francisco, you will continue to become more self assured. Your material may expand far beyond your thirty minutes. At this point, you may be able to headline at smaller clubs around the area. You can use your hometown clubs for headlining references and your middle slots at the large San Francisco clubs as quality references. You might not be making much more than a middle act's salary, but you will be able to put that title "HEADLINER" next to your name. It certainly looks good in the bio. Many of the larger clubs have

invented a new level of achievement called the "co-headliner" bill. This is essentially using two top middle acts who are not quite ready to pull a full forty five to fifty minute set, but who together can fill out a good show. The two co-headliners are given set times shorter than headliners, but longer than middle acts. Throughout the week, they alternate in the middle and headlining positions and take turns closing the week's shows. This is a great test of your abilities as a potential headliner. It's up to you to insure that the show closes strong! If you can do a great thirty-five minute set with a very strong close, you won't be middling or co-headlining for long.

When you go back to your favorite rooms on the road, let the bookers know of your achievements. Offer to co-headline, or possibly to headline for a trial basis. Just like you started low on the opening act and middle act pay scales and worked your way up with each succeeding appearance, you'll no doubt end up doing the same at the headlining position. If you prove yourself as a headliner, naturally you'll move up this pay scale too. Soon, you'll have a large list of national clubs you've headlined for references. You're income will steadily increase. You'll receive more and more stage time, which even at this late date is still valuable. You'll continue regular writing habits to force your material to expand and become even sharper. It won't be long before you're headlining in San Francisco, Seattle or

Boston.

Right about this time, your Aunt Jim and Uncle Martha have seen your success and have decided to become comedians too. Those who laughed at you when you started are beginning to think that this comedy biz is something good after all. As a headliner, you're beginning to meet new comics who are just like you were years ago when you were just starting out. You're giving them the same advice that others gave you at the start of your career. Everything seems to be going full circle. Now you even get the nice room in the comedy condo. Slowly but surely, you're becoming recognized locally and nationally as a headliner. Every month, you're adding another club to your headlining list. Bookers are telling each other that you are capable of pulling off a good headlining spot. The quality relationship that you've had with bookers from the earliest moments of your career is really starting to pay-off now. You're gaining a solid reputation throughout the industry. You're now headlining in San Francisco ... and Los Angeles is beginning to ask questions about you.

Cities like San Francisco or Boston, who have a rapidly expanding comedy community, have a reputation that is growing so rapidly that some TV shows such as The Tonight Show and Late Night with David Letterman are beginning to send out scouts to investigate. You may find yourself auditioning for the national spotlight and not setting foot anywhere near Los Angeles. If you do happen to get an invitation to audition for a national TV show, don't get overly excited about it. These shows view hundreds of performers every week and they are looking for very specific qualities. You may be a good comic, but you're just not what they're looking for at the present time. They may want to see how well you perform in the jungles of New York or L.A. before they think of booking you. Even at this level in your career, you may still be "a little green" to them. Don't worry if you're turned down at this stage. Chalk it up as a learning experience. Another chance will come along!

When headlining in a major city like San Francisco or Boston becomes routine, it's time to hit the big markets. It's finally time to move to L.A. or New York.

We tried to keep you away from this move earlier. From our experience, we've watched many young comics move to these areas way too soon in their careers and get swallowed up. In these markets, you're playing with the big guys! If you attempt to work in L.A. or New York too soon in your career, you may face terrible consequences further down the road. For example, auditioning for bookers in L.A. before you're truly ready might brand you and leave a mark that may be difficult to remove. If you walk in boasting that you're a hilarious comic and then perform ten minutes that an opening act would walk away from, you'll seriously scar your reputation with the booker. When you come back two years later with a set that is a thousand times better, you may do great with the audience, but the booker will still look at you as someone who just isn't ready. Had you built up your act on The Road or in the middle markets and established yourself as a headliner or a strong co-headliner, the results would have been different. You would have made a much better impression on the booker. Remember that you've been working at this comedy thing for years now. There are hundreds of comics walking the streets in these areas waiting for a break who are as good as or better than you! Don't blow a big chance by rushing an important audition before you're ready.

Break into these markets slowly. Try to book a club in an outlying area first. More than likely, you'll have to settle for a middle slot for lower pay than what you're normally accustomed to, but what

Comic Interview: Diane Nichols

How long have you been in comedy?
    12 years
What comics influenced you?
    Steve Allen, Mort Sahl, Jay Leno
Any advice for a new comic?
    Don't ask people who aren't comics for advice ... in fact,
    go to open mikes alone or with other comics.
What makes you a funny person?
    "Why do people laugh in church?" They hear two
    dialogues where most only hear one.
How has comedy benefited you?
    Comedy is an alternative viewpoint. It's validated
    my viewpoint.
What is the future of comedy?
    Comedy has become the new rock and roll. Rock heroes
    have always been hip and cool. However, the art of comedy
    should never be hip and cool ... you lose the real artists. Go
    watch the best ones work over and over. Don't be too
    influenced by the audience's acceptance of hacks.

the heck! The gig will pay your expenses and give you a chance to prove yourself in a major market. Once you've arranged your booking, call up the major clubs like The Comedy Store, Improvisation or The Comedy / Magic Club and inquire about open mike nights. Yes, open mike nights. You're back to square one, aren't you. Try to get scheduled on an open mike the week you're performing in the area. If you're successful in landing a spot, do your homework. Look at your material and pick out the ten most killer minutes of comedy you have. Your intent is to give the club everything you've got.

The open mike night you've booked will certainly bring back memories. It's exactly the same as your first open mike was except for one detail. The performers here are some of the best in the business and the quality of the evening's comedy will be extremely high.It's

very likely that major comics will filter in during the evening bumping the schedule to work on upcoming "Carson sets." Other comics might be working on new material. You might be lucky to get a midnight slot or even get on stage before last call. You may end up performing to ten people. But you'll *gain the experience*. Even though the entire booking staff has gone home long before they had a chance to see you, you can still know the feeling of performing at a club like The Comedy Store. You'll get the excitement of being on stage at a club like the Improv. Remember these feelings for your next opportunity. The next time you have a chance to perform at these major venues, your nervousness will be minimal. You'll remember the feelings of your first appearance. You'll remind yourself that these "hallowed grounds" for stand-up comedy are basically just like any other comedy club. Once you hit the stage, you're looking at a mike stand, a microphone and an audience ... exactly the same set-up that you've always had. By working your first appearance at these major venues in late slots in front of nobody, you'll have the chance to break down the illusion of grandeur that these clubs have enjoyed in your imagination. The next time that you perform here, you'll feel like this is just another club!

The notoriety that clubs like The Comedy Store and The Improvisation have received is not totally warranted. Although these are major venues and many comics have used them as springboards to great careers, every year it is becoming more and more evident that there are other paths to success for comics besides working at these two clubs. If for some reason you're not able to book yourself into their rotation, it's not the end of the line. Many comedians have gone on to great things despite having limited Comedy Store or Improv experience. While these clubs do enjoy a high industry profile, they do not necessarily make or break a career.

Just like in any other region of the country, if you've been successful at your initial week-long middle slot, you will no-doubt get offers for a re-booking. Co-headlining might be a possibility here. But remember, this is one of the top comedy areas in the country. The scale of talent trying to book stage time into Southern California or New York clubs at the middle and headliner levels is staggering. You may have headlined elsewhere, but in these towns, you may be *lucky* to middle!

With persistance, talent and luck, you will eventually move further up the comedy ladder, even in these major cities! You'll headline one or two places and before you know it, you'll be recognized as a full-fledged, no holes barred, out and out HEAD-LINER! This can only happen by playing lots of big city clubs and getting lots of stage time.

To be practical in acquiring this massive amount of big city stage time, you will again have to make a move. Just like you moved to a middle market to get closer to the action in those areas, now you'll have to pull up stakes again. Your improved professional comedy status of working headliner gigs on The Road across the country will increase your salary and offer you a chance to afford life in these high cost of living areas. Timing again is important. Be intelligent about your decision. Don't move until you're sure you can handle the expenses.

The grandest misconception about living and working in the L.A. or New York areas is the salary that clubs offer. As we mentioned earlier, even though the cost of living is excruciatingly high, local clubs ... even the biggest in the national comedy spotlight ... pay the same as, if not considerably less than, any other comedy club in the country. This combined with the amount of comics lining up for stage time does not present a very rosy economic future for a struggling comic who wants to perform exclusively in a major comedy center. At this point, your club schedule on The Road is more important than ever! By now you're commanding top dollar in national comedy clubs and it's paying the bills in L.A. You'll find yourself limiting your road schedule to perhaps half a month to make some money, and then performing the other half of the month around town looking for influential exposure. A strong balance between staying in town, gaining influential exposure by playing big city clubs for nothing, and hitting the road monthly to pay the bills must by found for the best possible chance for success and survival.

Managers and Agents

Obtaining a manager and agent is sometimes recommended at this point. Many times these two positions can possess two totally different functions. An agent is solely interested in booking you into the nicest venues for the top dollar. A manager is interested in guiding your career ... helping you pick the right projects to define the best image for you. By this time you've begun to find it easy to headline big city clubs and you've discovered that you're in demand all over the country. You have reached a level of success where you might need professional help in the way of managers and agents to help you plan a career. Finding the right personnel to fill these functions can be a very tricky business. The biggest in the industry are not necessarily the best for you and the smallest are not to be taken lightly.

You'll find certain similarities between seeking out a quality manager and auditioning for comedy clubs. In essence, you and the potential manager are auditioning each other. The manager is looking at you for talent and marketable possibilities while you are examining the manager for their level of trust, ability and competency. If and when you link up with someone who you feel can help you in your career, consider signing up. However, be very careful. If contracts are involved, seek out legal council for approval. Don't sign a document with anyone without investigating their reputation. Don't commit yourself to a fast-talking schmuck who tells you that you're the greatest thing since cheese-whiz and says he's gonna make you a star. These Barnum and Bailey types are quite dangerous.

For the time being, at least, it is recommended that you stick with a manager who perhaps is at a similar level in industry stature as you are. You're a headliner, but not a "star." They're managing headliners, but not "stars." Perhaps with your talent and your manager's increasingly important connections, the two of you will in time build *both* of your respective careers into successful ones.

A major mistake that many comics and performers make is immediately seeking out the biggest agency in the industry for booking representation. Don't look for a credibility problem with these companies ... certainly they are the most important and influential establishments in the business. It's a matter of clout. Sure you're talented. You're also very new by industry standards. A large firm might consider representing you and you may find yourself paying large sums of money for their services while wondering when the phone will start ringing. However, this lack of attention is not the fault of the agency. Besides yourself, they are handling many other performers. They may be handling major stars in the entertainment field. They will certainly spend more time promoting them rather than you. Stay with these firms if you're willing to wait at the bottom of the totem pole, but if you want more attentive help, look for an agency that is handling other performers similar to you in industry stature.

The trick is to find the proper manager / agent personnel whom you believe will have the time and the initiative to do the most for you. These individuals will be taking a percentage of your income so they will have a vested interest in seeing that you work regularly. No matter what level of industrial prestige they may enjoy, if you can find people who are fair, who believe in you and who are willing to give you all they can to help you in your career, your search is at an end.

A good agent will keep you working on the road regularly. While you're out of town, your manager will be busy lining up auditions for you to make when you get home. Chances are remote that you'd ever get any important auditions without formal representation. New 8 X 10's, updated bios and videos will certainly be needed by this point, but your manager will have a professional opinion on how you should be presented. You are the package they are trying to sell. Let them wrap it up properly. If they are a quality manager, they'll build the package that best represents you to the industry.

With professional representation, you will now again get a chance to showcase for national TV shows. This audition will be quite different from your previous experience. Now you have a manager who is selling you to the producers. When they finally see your act again, they will recognize you as an individual performer who has been recommended and promoted professionally, not as one comic in a group of twenty. This is surely a nice plus and a great basis for a showcase, but it won't insure a successful audition. Your manager

will arrange for the producers to see you at the club. You'll be advised that they'll be watching you. You'll probably be just as nervous as the first night you performed. Try to realize that this is just one of potentially unlimited opportunities. If this one fails, it's not the end of the world. There will be others. Very few comics are scheduled on national shows from one audition. Producers may want to see you several times over the course of a year before they decide if you're ready and your material is up to their standards. Your best hope is to present yourself professionally and give them the favorable impression that you're talented and improving all the time.

Before agreeing to network auditions, you should ask yourself if you're ready. *READY?* You've been performing for years and you have to ask yourself *THAT* question at this late stage? Just as on every other stage of The Comedy Ladder, the truth is that you don't want to step up too soon. Make sure of two points before attempting an audition for national TV. First, make sure your material is clean. Second, make sure you have enough of it.

Remember way back six or seven chapters ago when we recommended to always develop clean material. Hopefully, you've taken our advice. For if you have, by now you've developed a good amount of clean material that will work well on TV. As unfair as it may seem, if you do twenty minutes of "Dick Jokes" at your audition, it's adios as far as network TV goes. Your cleaner routines, labeled "TV Material," will be the variable that you as a performer will be measured by.

Not only must your material be clean, it has to be of exceptional quality. Just because some bits are successful in comedy clubs doesn't necessarily guarantee that they'll impress the producers. You can't expect to get on The Tonight Show by performing a twenty minute audition consisting of asking patrons what their names are and what they do for a living. TV producers are looking for fresh, original material. Your routines must have a special quality that excites them. At the very least, you must show enough potential that they will want to see you again at a later date.

You must also have a *good amount* of quality TV material. Many successful comics who've performed for years and have built reputations as national headliners have put off auditioning for network TV. The reason is simple. TV eats up good material. A standard "TV Comedy Set" consists of about six to eight minutes of stage time. You're performing in front of a mass audience. This audience hears the joke, responds and that's it. Once a joke has been performed on national TV, it's use to you as far as any future TV spot goes is minimal. Each time you appear on network TV, you're expected to have a different six to eight minute set of absolutely hilarious new material. It's not like the comedy clubs where you can get away with performing the same show every night.

If you happen to be a huge success in your first appearance on a show, it's not unlikely that you'll get an instant re-booking ... possibly scheduled as soon as several days after your initial appearance. Some network shows have scheduling complications that turn up instantly. Sometimes they get performer cancellations. It's been a common practice to use comics as replacements. If you're fresh on their minds from your first successful set, they may have you back very soon for an encore performance to fill the gap. You'd better be ready with a fresh set of six to eight minutes of good TV material for your next appearance.

There are so many examples of comics who've performed their best material in their first network TV appearance and unfortunately bomb on their follow-up spot. They rushed it. They should have waited until they had enough material to fill several TV Comedy Sets before attempting the first one. It will be awhile before the producers book them again.

Comic Interview: Pat Paulsen

How long have you been in comedy?
        40 years
What comics influenced you?
        Victor Borge, Bob and Ray
Any advice for a new comic?
        We need more old comics.
What makes you a funny person?
        Probably looks, delivery and timing.
How has comedy benefited you?
        Fucked me up, but I made a lot of money,
        which I pissed away.
What is the future of comedy?
        Comedy should be banned from serious
        conversations.
Any additional comments?
        Don't run for president. That's MY angle.

Unfortunately, network TV is not what it used to be. There was a day when variety shows flourished on television. Today, "The Tonight Show" and "Late Night with David Letterman" are basically the dream gigs for comics. Not only are the odds of appearing on these two shows tough, the fact that they are guided by the same production company makes it additionally difficult. It's possible you may not be liked by either production staff. What to do now? There may be one or two other network shows available for work, but truly, Cable TV is the comic's godsend! Stand-up comedy is very popular on cable at the present time. HBO, Showtime and other networks are frequently doing comedy specials with stand-ups. The audiences for these shows don't match the commercial network's numbers for their top programs, but they do have the benefit of multiple repeat showings. Naturally, the standards of acceptable TV material are less stringent on cable. However, this doesn't mean go for the dick jokes. Producers for these shows aren't looking for comics who can do the raunchiest set and get the cheapest laugh. They want comedy that is intelligent, bright and ORIGINALLY FUNNY just like the network producers do. You may be able to add the occasional FuckShitDickTits here and there, but, again, if your material can't stand alone without them, the producers will probably stand without you. Your auditions for these networks should be no different than those of commercial TV. If the jokes are there, you'll make a favorable impression.

TV. Films. National recognition. Very few performers reach this level of success in comedy. However, the beauty of the business, and perhaps the most attractive thing about it, is that this level is potentially accessible to anyone with considerable talent, intelligence and patience.

Throughout this chapter you've probably imagined a certain image in your mind every time we've mentioned "The Comedy Ladder." Maybe you've thought of it as a long, tall structure reaching high into the clouds. You couldn't even see the top of it. Well that's part of what we had in mind. However, there is one dimension of the ladder that you might not have thought about. While the ladder is tall and reaches unseen rewards, it also starts at the bottom quite wide. You'll find as you climb it that the ladder becomes skinnier and skinnier. Thousands of comics start at the bottom of the ladder and it's wide enough to accomodate everyone! You'll notice as you continue climbing that there's less and less room on each succeeding rung! You'll see other comics stall on lower levels or fall off completely. By the time that you can finally see the top, the room on the ladder has reduced to a size that can hold only a fraction of the original performers!

Your talent will help you hold your position on The Comedy Ladder. Your creativity, your patience and your hustle will see that you continue climbing.

Chapter Nine:
The Punch Line

Aunt Jim and Uncle Martha are soooooo proud of you now! You're the pride of the family. "Hey lookie here" ... "We've got a celebrity in the family!!!" Even your dad has started to show you some respect. Sure he paid for four years of college. Sure you studied medicine and could perform open heart surgury if you had the motivation. Sure you threw it all away to tell jokes about Ford Escorts. What the hell! You're making five times the money he makes. You can send HIM to college now.

The life of a successful top entertainer can be unique. Suddenly you're like a visitor to another planet to your old friends. People you knew for years before you ever stepped on stage seem to act so different now. They're just getting used to having to share you with the rest of the world.

Consider this book as an elaborate set-up for your career. Consider the rewards ... the fruits of your labor ... the Punch Line. It's the pay off. The reason for getting into stand-up in the first place. Like any joke you might tell on stage, the punch line is only as powerful as the set-up that preceeds it. We sincerely hope that this book will contribute to a powerful set-up.

Every stage of your career will bring with it a certain level of accomplishment. Satisfaction and pride can be gained with every achievement, no matter how small. The only way you'll make it in comedy is realizing that the pay off, or "Punch Line" isn't just at the top of The Comedy Ladder. Every level you climb has its rewards. It's recognizing these rewards that keeps the comics you see at comedy clubs around the country performing nightly. The ongoing achievements keep them going.

Throughout this book, we've given you what we think is a well thought out plan for success in the field of comedy. We've been able to gather this information from our years of experience in the comedy business. Each time we've described a different situation in this book, we could come up with a long list of comic's names who've had to deal with similar situations in the past.

We've seen comics on every step of The Comedy Ladder. We've watched many rise from opening acts to major stars. Case in point: Garry Shandling. Garry was the first comedian we ever put on our stage. He filled the opening slot for our debut week. At the time, 1980 to be exact, he was doing middle slots around the country. He offered to open for us to give us a good start. He did and our start was very good indeed. Very soon afterwards, we were proud to headline him. He felt particularly grateful because we were one of the few clubs at the time who were willing to take a chance to give him the headline spot. Garry's talent was so immense, his material so sharp, that he soon found himself on national TV. He was ready. He had worked hard to develop not one, but two headliner length sets of material to work from, most of it clean, ideal TV material. His initial TV appearances did indeed come in rapid succession. He was prepared. His success appeared to come out of nowhere, but in actuality his many years of comedy club work would insure that he would never be branded as an "overnight success." Today, of course, he's a major star, but he still no doubt subscribes to the same hard working habits that he developed as an up and coming comic. That dedication will continue his success.

Comic Interview: Dennis Wolfberg

How long have you been in comedy?
> 9 years

What comics influenced you?
> There are different kinds of comics I've admired for different reasons. Woody Allen (comic genius for movie making and stand-up), Buddy Hacket (saloon humor), Victor Borge (comedy and music), Jackie Gleason and Peter Sellers (comedic acting), Steve Martin (zany comedy), Robin Williams (improvisation), Johnny Carson (TV comedy) and Rodney Dangerfield (joke machine). Everyone you admire has an influence, which when combined with your own personality, comes up with your own unique package.

Any advice for a new comic?
> Work, work, work! Comedy, like any other craft, requires honing whatever talent you have. The more you work, the better you'll hone it. No tennis player ever became a champion without spending hours and hours on the court. Be willing to take chances and be willing to fail. Tape every set and listen to your work. Video tape and watch your work.

What makes you a funny person?
> People have always laughed at me as long as I can remember. My family certainly didn't discourage me. Rather than being seen and not heard, they encouraged anything I happened to say. They frequently laughed too! So somehow I thought I was funny because people were laughing.

How has comedy benefited you?
> It's been greatly fulfilling. Last night after the first show, a gentleman came up to me and, having sat through my show, realized that he had forgotten how to laugh. He had gotten so involved with life's various pressures, forces and tragedies that he'd lost his ability to enjoy himself and he thanked me for making him laugh again. It doesn't get any better than that!

Any additional comments?
> I taught school for three years and did late night comedy sometimes at two or three in the morning in front of two or three generally intoxicated people. After 1980, I took a leave of absence to apply my comedic trade full time. For new comics, don't get discouraged. Give yourself two or three years before you're willing to sit down and take stock as to whether you have a future. If the desire to perform comedy is still not burning within you, I would suggest forget it. Performing comedy comes from an insatiable need.- "I need to go on stage, I need to be funny, I need to hear those laughs" - otherwise you have pretty little chance, I believe.

If you read our chapter on The Comedy Ladder and you happen to think *"Hey this is all fine and good, but what if my home is in LA already? Are you saying I should move to Frostbite Falls to start a career?"*

No. That's probably not necessary. But you should consider working in clubs outside of a major comedy center first. Take the time to learn your craft. When you're ready, begin to play the clubs in L.A. The only difference between you and the other comics is that you won't have to drive as far to get home.

You might be asking yourself *"Hey I went to a club last night and saw a hilarious comic. He had the crowd on the floor. He was killing! His twenty minute bit on penis sizes was a scream!"*

That's great. Let's see him do it on Carson.

"Wait a minute. What about Cable?"

When HBO does a comedy special about male sex organs, he'll be the first they call.

"I've been doing comedy for five weeks and I've got three hours of great stuff!"

Face it pal. If you've got three minutes of quality stuff, it would be great.

"What's wrong with stealing material? How does any comic get started without it? How does anyone know I didn't write it first?"

Here. Take this pistol and give some mouth to mouth.

"Hey I can't stand being an opening act anymore. When am I going to start moving up?"

Nobody said there was a time limit for any given level of

success. The only answer is keep working. Change your act around a bit until you find a formula that starts clicking. We know performers that were nervous opening acts for years. They continued to work hard on their material and they made some adjustments. All of a sudden, their careers shot up like rockets!

"I'm still not making any money at this business. I'm getting good spots. I'm middling regularly. I'm still not seeing any cash!"

Try being a little more aggressive with bookers. If you feel that you can't work for the offered pay, nobody said you have to take the job. Maybe your stand will convince the booker to give you more money next time.

"Bookers just aren't moving me up fast enough!"

Like we told the last guy, be a little more aggressive next time. Take a stand. Tell them that you can't open any more. You have to middle. If the booker sees that your improved act and material warrant the change, they'll be happy to move you up.

"I do the best Jack Nicholson impression in the country and nobody's giving me any work!"

EVERYBODY'S DOING JACK NICHOLSON!

"Andy Rooney?"

DITTO.

"Ed Sullivan?"

LEAVE THE ROOM!

"I've been working for years at comedy. I've written lots of good clean material. It's all original. It gets good laughs. I try to act

as professional as possible in all of my business dealings. I consis-
tantly tape my sets and improve my act. I'm willing to make the
necessary sacrifices to make it in comedy."

We'll see you at the top!

The following is a
partial listing of
comedy clubs as
recommended by
several professional
comics.

THE COMEDY CLUB
430 Green Springs Hwy No. 28
Homewood, Alabama (205) 942-0008

THE COMEDY CLUB
1407-14 N. Memorial Pkwy,
Huntsville, Alabama (205)536-3329

FINNY BONES
The Days Inn Hotel; 502 W. Camel-
back,
Phoenix, Arizona (602) 234-1717

THE IMPROV
930 E. University D1-201
Tempe, Arizona (602) 921-9877

**LAFF'S COMEDY NIGHTCLUB
AND CAFFE**
The Village on Broadway; 2900 E.
Broadway,
Tucson, Arizona (602) 32-FUNNY

THE COMEDY HOUSE
Breckenridge Village
Little Rock, Arkansas (501) 221-2004

LAUGHS UNLIMITED
7630 Greenback Lane,
Citrus Heights, California (916) 969-
1076

L.A. CABARET
17271 Ventura Blvd.
Encino, California (818) 501-3737

COMEDY AND MAGIC CLUB
1018 Hermosa Avenue,
Hermosa Beach, California (213) 372-
1193

THE COMEDY STORE
8433 W. Sunset Blvd.
Hollywood, California (213) 650-
6268

THE IMPROVISATION
4255 Campus Drive,
Irvine, California (714) 854-5459

THE COMEDY CLUB
49 S. Pine and Ocean,
Long Beach, California (213)437-
5326

IGBY'S
11637 Tennessee Place
Los Angeles, California (213) 477-
3553

THE LAFF STOP
2122 SE Bristol,
Newport Beach, California (415) 796-
5700

THE IMPROV
832 Garnet Avenue,
Pacific Beach, California (619)483-
4522

LAUGHS UNLIMITED
1124 Firehouse Alley,
Sacramento, CA (916) 446-5905

THE COMEDY ISLE
The Bahia Resort;
998 West Mission Dr.,
San Diego, California

COBBS COMEDY CLUB
The Cannery; 2801 Leavenworth,
San Francisco, California (415) 928-
4320

THE HOLY CITY ZOO
408 Clement Street,
San Francisco, California (415) 386-4242

THE IMPROVISATION
401 Mason Street,
San Francisco, California (415) 441-7787

THE PUNCH LINE
444 Battery Street,
San Francisco, California (415) 474-3801

TOMMY T'S
150 West Juana,
San Leandro, California (415) 351-LAFF

ROOSTER T. FEATHERS
157 W. El Camino Real,
Sunnyvale, California (408) 736-0921

THE COMEDY WORKS
1226 15th Street,
Denver, Colorado (303) 595-3637

GOVERNOR'S COMEDY SHOP
56 West Park Place,
Stamford, Connecticut (203) 324-3117

WILMINGTON COMEDY CLUB
410 Market Street.,
Wilmington, Deleware (302) 652-6873

UNCLE FUNNY'S COMEDY CLUB
6000 N. Federal Hwy.,
Ft. Lauderdale, Florida (305) 491-4423

GOVERNOR'S COMEDY SHOP
3001 East Commercial Blvd.
Ft. Lauderdale, Florida (407) 776-JOKE

BONKERS COMEDY CLUB
4315 N. Orange Blossom Tr.,
Orlando, Florida (407) 298-BONK

COCONUTS COMEDY CLUB
in the Holiday Inn Airport; 7250 N. Tamiami Tr.,
Sarasota, Florida (813) 355-2781

PUNCH LINE
3250 North Lake Parkway,
Atlanta, Georgia (404) 493-3949

NUTS COMEDY CABARET
620 West Idaho,
Boise, Idaho (208) 336-2255

THE IMPROVISATION
504 N. Wells St.,
Chicago, Illinois (312) 527-2500

BROAD RIPPLE COMEDY CLUB
6281 North College Avenue,
Indianapolis, Indiana (317)255-4211

INDIANAPOLIS COMEDY CONNECTION
247 South Meridan Street,
Indianapolis, Indiana (317) 631-3536

PEPPERONI'S COMEDY CLUB
El Fredo's Pizza; 523 W. 19th Street,
Sioux City, Iowa (712) 258-0691

SLAPSTIX COMEDY CLUB
2120 N. Woodlawn #352,
Wichita, Kansas

THE FUNNY FARM
The Mid-City Mall; 1250 Bardstown
Rd.,
Louisville, Kentucky (502) 459-0022

SLAPSTIX
2222 Clearview Pkwy, Suite G,
Mattairie, Louisiana (504) 454-0052

SLAPSTIX
The Brokerage; 34 Market Place,
Baltimore, Maryland (301) 383-7527

CATCH A RISING STAR
30 JFK Street, Harvard Square,
Cambridge, Massachusetts (617) 661-9887

MAINSTREET COMEDY SHOW-CASE
314 E. Liberty,
Ann Arbor, Michigan (313) 996-9080

CHAPS ON MAIN
105 E. Michigan,
Kalamazoo, Michigan (616) 343-3922

COMEDY GALLERY
Riverplace; 25 Main Street,
SE Minneapolis, Minnesota (612)
331-JOKE

SLAPSTIX
1148 W. 103rd Street,
Kansas City, Missouri (816) 941-YUKS

STANFORD AND SONS COMEDY HOUSE
504 Westport Rd.,
Kansas City, Missouri (816) 753JOKE

THE ROYAL GROVE NIGHTCLUB
304 W. Cornhusker Hwy.,
Lincoln, Nebraska (402) 477-2026

CATCH A RISING STAR
Bally's Casino Resort,
3645 Las Vegas Blvd.,
Las Vegas, Nevada (702) 739-4397

THE IMPROVISATION
The Rivera Hotel; 2901 Las Vegas
Blvd. S.,
Las Vegas, Nevada

THE IMPROVISATION
Resort International Hotel
Atlantic City, (609) 340-6830

CATCH A RISING STAR
Hyatt Regency Princeton,
Princeton, New Jersey (609) 987-1234

LAFF'S COMEDY NIGHT CLUB
3100-A Juan Tabo Blvd. NE.,
Albuquerque, New Mexico (505) 296-JOKE

ROUTE 66 COMEDY CLUB
4100 Central SE,
Albuquerque, New Mexico (505) 266-3007

CAROLINES AT THE SEAPORT
89 South Street on Pier 17
New York, New York (212)233-4900

CATCH A RISING STAR
1487 First Avenue,
New York, New York (212) 794-1906

THE IMPROVISATION
358 West 44th Street,
New York, New York (212)765-8268

YUK YUK'S KOMEDY KABARET
150 Andrews Place,
Rochester, New York (716) 325-4088

CHARLIE GOODNIGHTS
861 W. Morgan Street
Raleigh, North Carolina (919) 833-8356

CLEVELAND COMEDY CLUB
2230 E. 4th Street,
Cleveland, Ohio (216) 781-7735

THE IMPROVISATION
2000 Sycamore Level 1,
Cleveland, Ohio (216) 696-4677

THE COMEDY WORKS
126 Chestnut Street,
Philadelphia, Pennsylvania (215) WACKY-97

THE FUNNY BONE COMEDY CLUB
221 South Street, Abbot Square,
Philadelphia, Pennsylvania (215) 440-9670

THE FUNNY BONE COMEDY CLUB
The Shops at Station Square,
Pittsburg, Pennsylvania (410) 281-3130

THE PUNCH LINE
115 Pelham Road,
Greenville, South Carolina (803) 235-5233

THE COMEDY CATCH
3224 Brainerd Rd.,
Chattanooga, Tennessee (615) 629-2233

THE FUNNY PAGE
5771 Brainerd Rd.,
Chattanooga, Tennessee (615) 892-6667

THE COMEDY HOUSE
4095 America Way,
Memphis, Tennessee (901) 366-7711

SIR LAFS-A-LOT
535 S. Highland.,
Memphis, Tennessee (901) 324-JOKE

ZANIES COMEDY SHOWPLACE
2025 8th Avenue South,
Nashville, Tennessee (615) 269-0221

THE IMPROV
9810 North Central,
Dallas, Texas (214) 750-5866

COMEDY SHOWCASE
12547 Gulf Freeway,
Houston, Texas (713) 481-1188

THE PUNCH LINE
Marritt Westloop Galleria;
1750 Westloop,
Houston, Texas (713) 960-0111

COMEDY CLUB
at the Thouroughgood Inn;
4520 Independence Blvd,
Virginia Beach, Virginia (804) 499-7071

THE COMEDY UNDERGROUND
at Swannies; 222 S. Main,
Seattle, Washington (206) 622-9353

COMEDY CAFE
1520 K Street, NW
Washington, D.C. (202) 638-JOKE

Here's a few of our friends in comedy with whom we've had the pleasure of doing business. Working closely with these talented professionals makes it a pleasure to be a part of this industry.

Milt Abel
Robert Aguayo
Carlos Alazraqui
Jimmy Aleck
Paul Alexander
Neal Alexander
Elaine Allison
Jeff Altman
Amazing Jonathan
Harry Anderson
Fred Anderson
Dave Anderson
Karen Anderson
Dave Atkinson
Kenny Aubrey
Stephen B.
Mike Bailey
Bruce Baum
Ngaio Bealum
Phil Beauman
Rob Becker
Tim Bedore
Ross Bennett
Bentoni
Joel Berman
Dennis Bertsch
Moe Betterman
Cody Blaine
Jon Boggs
Bill Bonner
Lois Bromfield
Larry Brown
Steve Bruner
Jimmy Burns
Irv Burton
Derrick Cameron
John Carfi

John Carney
Dana Carvey
Brian Catalina
Vince Champ
Cal Clarke
Rick Clay
Brian Copeland
Dave Coulier
Joe Crown
Brad Cummings
Terry Dadd
Robin Davies
Eric Davis
Evan Davis
May Lee Davis
JoAnn Dearing
Jeff DeHart
Peter DePaula
Destiny
Brian Diamond
Ken Diaz
Bob Dubac
Julia Duffy
Dave Dugan
Will Durst
Tony Edwards
Billy Elmer
Bill Enguall
Mark Eubanks
Maria Falzone
Jim Farrell
Chuck Fayne
David Feldman
Lamont Ferguson
Michael Finney
Mike Flannery
John Fox

Dennis Franklin
Jack Gallagher
Ken Garr
Peter Gaulke
Bobby Gaylor
Mark George
Eric Gerrard
Howie Gold
Reno Goodale
Great Scott
Dawn Greene
Jimmy Gunn
Sam Guttman
Ray Hanna
Jeannene Hansen
Ed Hart
Sue Healy
John Henton
Don Hepner
Scott Herriott
George Hirschman
Bill Hicks
Rene Hicks
Chris Hobbs
Brian Holtzman
Tyler Horn
James Wesley
Jackson
Rob Jacobson
Jeff Jena
Jake Johansen
Edmund Johnson
Jay Johnson
Denny Johnston
Tim Jones
Jennie Jones
Jaz Kaner

Alan Kaye
Paul Kelly
Ronny Kenny
Lori Kilmartin
Andy Kindler
Ken King
Pete Kirby
Susan Kolinski
Jeremy Kramer
Steve Kravitz
Stephanie Landers
Mike Larson
Howard Leff
Jay Leno
Brian Leonard
Ellis Levinson
Martin Lewis
Mike Lipton
Randy Lubas
Al Lubel
Frank Lunny
Mack and Jamie
Mike Mancini
Henriette Mantel
Jack Marion
Tom Martin
Edie Mathews
Shamus McCool
Jimmy McGee
Mike McKea
Brian McKim
Tom McTigue
Kevin Meany
Larry Miller
Mark Miller
Dennis Miller
Jerry Miller

Kelly Monteith
Paul Mooney
Steve Moore
Danny Mora
Dan Morgan
Joe Morris
Gary Mule Deer
Barry Neal
Kevin Nealon
Diane Nichols
Joe Nipote
O'Brien and Valdez
Tim O'Rourke
Carey Odes
Dave Pokorny
John Pate
Pat Paulsen
Emo Philips
Daily Pike
Turk Pipkin
Mark Pitta
Kevin Pollack
Paula Poundstone
Frank Prinzi
Chris Raines
Willie Randolph
Johnny Ray
Carla Rea
Ron Reid
Joe Restivo
Carl Reye
Rick Reynolds
Dave Richards
Mike Rivera
Ron Robertson
Paul Robins
Rick Rockwell

Kevin Rooney
Tim Rose
Jeff Ross
Bob Saget
Angel Salazar
Bobby Salem
Roger Scheideman
Dave Schueber
Rob Schneider
Barbara Scott
Jerry Seinfeld
Stan Sellers
Ken Severa
Garry Shandling
Nicky Shane
Thom Sharpe
Barbara Shaw
Mark Schiff
Bob Shimmel
Wil Shriner
Jose Simon
Larry Skinner
Bobby Slayton
Bruce Smirnoff
Yakov Smirnoff
Steve Smith
Carrie Snow
Barry Sobel
Ed Soloman
Doug Starks
Johnny Steele
Jovanka Steele
Chicago Steve
Lynn Stobener
Dave Strassman
Glen Super
Mark Taylor

Rufus Taylor
Tree
Grant Turner
Willie Tyler and
Lester

Vacarl
Del Van Dyke
George Wallace
Don Ware
Jeff Wayne
Dan Wedeking

Peter Wick
Matt Weinhold
Tim Wiggins
Terry Wilkerson
Larry Wilson
Michael Winslow
Dennis Wolfberg
Bob Worley
Kim Worth
Robert Wuhl